THE HOSTAGE

THE HOSTAGE

Christopher, son of the Danish Prime Minister, is kidnapped by Mr Møller, a political opponent who wants to take Denmark out of NATO. Unfortunately, Mr Møller's muddled idealism makes him play straight into the hands of the Red Brigade. They take Christopher *and* Mr Møller's son as hostage for his silence. When the terrorists fail in their ransom demand Christopher is only too aware that death will be the consequence and that they must escape.

Anne Holm established a brilliant international reputation with the publication of the award-winning *I am David*.

ANNE HOLM

The Hostage

Translated from the Danish by
PATRICIA CRAMPTON

MAMMOTH

First published in Great Britain 1980
by Methuen Children's Books Ltd
Magnet paperback edition published 1982
Reprinted 1982, 1984 and 1986
Published 1990 by Mammoth
an imprint of Mandarin Paperbacks
Michelin House, 81 Fulham Road, London SW3 6RB
Reprinted 1990, 1991

Mandarin is an imprint of the Octopus Publishing Group,
a division of Reed International Books Ltd

ISBN 0 7497 0370 9

A CIP catalogue record for this title
is available from the British Library

Printed in Great Britain
by Cox & Wyman Ltd, Reading, Berkshire

Also by Anne Holm

I AM DAVID
THE SKY GREW RED

The Hostage

1

The weather really was *miasmal*! Chris hunched his shoulders up to his ears and quickened his step, smiling slyly to himself. That would be his contribution to Father's vocabulary tonight: 'miasmal'. Old Skovmand had actually been using it for years, without his pupils' thinking of it as anything but a teacher's affectation – and so, since he had not thought of anything else for this evening, he had looked it up and found that it was a real word.

It was pitch-dark, but for the advertising signs, flashing their coloured lights on the street, all the way down the rain-soaked Jaegersborg Avenue; and it was blowing great guns, as well. Perhaps, if the Tystrups were out for dinner and had had no time to look before they went, he might be lucky and find some walnuts . . . unless Father had come home, of course! He was mad about walnuts and Mother always teased him, saying that he must have been a squirrel in a former life.

They were busy redecorating the windows at the bookshop – that was the only activity in the avenue, as the hot-dog salesman had already packed up and gone home. Well, who would be taking an evening walk in this weather? Chris turned the corner, ducking his head. There was always a violent gust of wind here and he could do nothing about his rumpled hair; Mother had been complaining about it again this morning, asking if he could not be persuaded to have a hair-cut.

Heaven knew, there was nothing he would like more, but he had enough trouble at school as it was, over Father . . . well, not in his class, but he could just hear the gang's feeble-minded comments from the parallel class, if he had a hair-cut . . . and he couldn't tell Mother that.

One of the faded wet leaves landed right in his face. It would be great to have sandwiches and hot tea now.

There was a car parked right outside the Tystrups' – there would be! So it was no good trying to look for fallen walnuts, after all.

'Good evening, Christopher. Er, you are Christopher Egstrup, aren't you?'

'Yes,' said Chris, rather surprised. The man who had apparently been sitting in the parked car was now coming towards him and had stopped under the street lamp. He was tall and thinnish, that was about all you could see in the dim light.

'My name is Mogens Møller . . . ah, you don't know me, but I was at a meeting with your father this evening and we arranged to go out for a bite of supper . . . your father picked up your mother, and we said *we* would wait for you.'

'Oh,' said Chris, disappointed. He had just been thinking how great it would be to come into the nice, warm living-room, with the light down over the table and the teacups and the big teapot, and the salami and the honey jar – and Mother, who would be doing the crossword and ready to listen to the events of the day. And instead of that, he was going to have to go out and be polite to strangers and get to bed late, so that it would be even more impossible to wake up in the morning.

Chris realized that he had not been particularly polite,

8

just saying 'Oh'. 'I mean, thank you, but I'd just like to wash my hands . . .'

'Never mind that,' said Mr Møller, 'you can do that at our house. We've been hanging about here for a quarter of an hour already.'

Well, yes, that was true enough; Chris said something polite about how extremely windy it was and followed the man to the car, trying not to feel irritated at being forced to be the guilty party . . . hang it, he hadn't asked to be waited for! But Father and Mother must have thought it would be fun for him to go, since they had arranged it . . . whoever Mr Møller might be.

There was another man in the car, sitting at the back. 'This is Torben,' said Mr Møller, and the man said 'Hallo'.

There was only a faint light for the few seconds while the car doors were open – Chris could make out that the other man was young and long-haired, while Mr Møller was more the usual age for a father. Then they were in the car and Mr Møller had started the engine. Chris asked where they were going. After all, you had to say something.

'Right to the back of beyond, northwards,' said Mr Møller; you could hear that he was smiling. Then he began to ask how things had gone that evening and he obviously knew something about chess, so some time passed in discussing it, as they made their way – rather too fast, in Chris's opinion – along the dark, empty suburban streets.

What adults said to children was seldom exciting enough to need all your attention; Chris was keeping an eye on the compass on his watch as he answered – covertly, of course. Luckily he had it on his right wrist, because he was left-handed, so if he held it below the level of his hip Mr Møller could not see it. They would have to turn soon, he thought, because they were still

9

heading directly westwards, although they were out of the town now.

That Torben in the back must be a bit of a dummy; he hadn't uttered a squeak up to now, apart from a stupid snigger when Mr Møller said they were going to the back of beyond. Perhaps he wasn't really grown up after all . . . perhaps he was Mr Møller's son; yes, that was it . . . he had only said 'Hallo', and adults who knew who Father was generally talked to Chris in a different way, not so casually.

Now Mr Møller sounded very decent, a bit nervous perhaps, as adults often did when they were alone with children they did not know, but at least not over-impressed. What were they nervous about? As if children were an unknown, dangerous race! He would soon be getting to that bit about 'What are you going to be when you grow up?' Yes, here it came!

'I really don't know,' said Chris. 'I'm only thirteen; Father and Mother say there's plenty of time for me to think about it, because I'm interested in so many different things and it's impossible to know which of them will last.'

It was extraordinary how much people thought they could ask children about their private affairs! As if you really wanted to cough up all the details of your plans, even if you had any! What would they say, if children they did not know at all calmly asked: 'What job do you do, sir?'

Chris had actually been on the point of asking aloud, but that would have been cheeky. After all, Mr Møller was only trying to entertain a boy to whom he wanted to be kind . . . even if it was obviously only for Father's sake.

They must have taken a couple of turnings, for now they were heading back eastwards again. Suddenly Chris felt a little lonely. It was so dark and wet out, and quite late, too, and here he sat, murmuring polite nothings to a strange man while his lovely bed retreated further and further – could Father and Mother have realized quite how far away Mr Møller lived?

He yawned.

'Are you sleepy, Christopher?'

'Oh, no.' Chris smiled back at the friendly face which was turned towards him for a moment, away from the wheel. What deep furrows it took on, in the dim light from the instrument panel!

He wasn't, either, it was just that he had suddenly felt rather alone. His father always said that he had inherited *his* sleepy head: 'As long as anger and worry and excitement only make you yawn, there's no danger of your getting into hot water,' he said, 'because you'll always be able to sleep on it before you act.'

'. . . actually, I'm almost always called Chris,' he said aloud.

Mr Møller remarked that that was a bit shorter, and turned into a driveway. Chris was wide awake at once. It would be good to see Father and Mother. Funny, actually, that they should have called him Christopher, to Mr Møller . . .

'Here we are then, my lad.'

Chris jumped out of the car and looked about him, not that one could see much in the darkness. A long, low house and a little courtyard, a few tall trees, right out in the country. But he should be able to see a car.

The hall was quite big and rather untidy. The man called Torben went through one door and Mr Møller opened another for Chris.

Chris walked through it and said to the lady who was sitting in the room, knitting: 'Where are my father and mother?'

He knew for certain that they were not there.

'Good evening, Christopher,' said the lady nervously. 'They're . . . they're coming soon. Come and have a cup of tea.'

'I don't believe you,' said Chris, staying where he was.

Mr Møller said irritably that: 'You might as well go in and why do you suddenly imagine that your parents are not coming?'

'They would have been here, in that case, wouldn't they? You said you had been waiting for a quarter of an hour till I came back from the Chess Club, and Father's driver would have been outside with the car already. And Father and Mother never call me Christopher to anyone they know.'

The lady put down her knitting and began to pour tea at the laid table; she was having difficulty in keeping the spout steady. 'It's . . . it's not my husband and me they know, Christopher. It's . . . it's some of your father's good friends, who . . . all this is just a game they're playing, you mustn't be frightened, my dear.'

'I'm not frightened,' said Chris slowly. 'But I don't think you should expect my father to think it's a very good joke.'

Mr Møller threw himself into a chair by the table. 'I damn well hope he does,' he laughed, taking the cup of tea which Mrs Møller handed him. 'Otherwise the others will have me to deal with.'

Chris sat down unwillingly and put sugar in the tea which was poured out for him. Mrs Møller offered him bread and butter, and there was ham too, and cheese. The fresh brown bread was good and he was certainly hungry, but all the same . . .

'Who are these friends?' he asked.

Mr Møller smiled again and said he had promised not to tell; he did not look as though he were really enjoying himself now. Nor did Mrs Møller, for that matter. Chris ate in silence, while Mr and Mrs Møller talked about her knitting and some wool which was the wrong colour. Then he came to a decision, wiped his fingers on the paper napkin and said:

'I don't want to be rude, Mr Møller, but I think it would be best if you drove me home at once. Father and Mother are not used to me being really late and I'm terribly bad at getting up in the morning.'

'Your father and mother know where you are, Chris, and I'm afraid I'm too tired to drag myself all the way back into town.' He spoke kindly enough, but in that kind of parental tone which means 'Not another word on that subject'. Before Chris could answer, Mrs Møller was on her feet. 'It's dreadful weather, too, and if you find it difficult to get up in the morning, you had better sleep here tonight, so you can go to bed now. Come on, I'll show you your room.'

Chris stifled a yawn. If he was not prepared to start making a fuss right away, or cry, or something, there was obviously nothing he could do – they were grown-ups, after all. But cripes, he was furious! It was all he could do to make himself say some kind of decent good-night to Mrs Møller, although it might not actually be the Møllers' fault, they were obviously already beginning to realize that this was a stupid game, to judge by the peculiar way they had been talking to each other downstairs.

But who on earth could have had such an idiotic idea? Worse than idiotic, in fact! His parents' real friends, the ones they had known since long before he was born, could not possibly have done it. Chris kicked off his shoes. But it couldn't be any of the others either, could it? Some of them were pretty dreary, but those were the very ones who were the least likely to think of something so childish, so utterly ridiculous, nothing remotely like a game.

13

Chris yawned again, tiptoed out on his stockinged feet to the bathroom and washed his hands; there was a toothbrush there, which Mrs Møller had seen to, and pyjamas as well. Chris lay down and switched off the light. His last thought before he fell asleep was a satisfied: 'Cripes, how wild Father and Mother are going to be!'

The window was in the wrong place. And the foot of the bed was absolutely the wrong height. Chris blinked his eyes a few times and reached out for his glasses – ah, *there* they were! Yes, but that picture wasn't usually there, was it?

He sat up in bed with a start, suddenly wide awake. He wasn't at home after all, he had spent the night with those crazy Møllers and . . . yes, what was the time? How on earth was he going to get to school on time?

He slid quietly out of bed, as you do when you are in a stranger's house and do not know their morning habits, and looked out of the window. There was the courtyard of the night before, with a garden beyond it and some fruit trees; it was pouring with rain. And there was not a house in sight, only big, bare fields, sloping gently into valleys, and far, far away, a wood. They hadn't even given him the least idea where they were – only that it was in North Zealand.

And every time he had looked at his compass the night before, it had shown anything but North . . .

Now there was someone on the stairs; Chris was back in bed, fast and silently, his back turned to the room and his eyes closed. He did not quite know why, but it was always so tiresome getting the day started, and today, on top of that, he was supposed to be awake enough to talk to these crazy strangers. Might as well put it off a little longer; after all he could not possibly get to school in time for the first lesson.

There was a slight sound at the door and someone came in. Chris held his breath; only later did he remember that in books people always breathed deeply and regularly when they wanted to convince someone they were asleep. Mrs Møller apparently didn't know, either, for she stood where she was for an endless moment, before tiptoeing out again.

It *had* been Mrs Møller: you could hear from the way she sighed. And now she was locking the blinking door!

Chris sat up in bed, snatched his glasses and stared at the door. Locked! What were they thinking of? For the first time he began to feel worried. Even for a bad joke, this was going too far; they couldn't really be mad, could they? No, they seemed a perfectly ordinary married couple, living in a perfectly ordinary house in the country.

She had not gone down again, but someone else was coming upstairs now. Chris crept out of bed, testing each step warily before he shifted his weight, because the floorboards might creak.

'He's still asleep,' said Mrs Møller's low voice on the other side of the door.

'You'd better wake him up,' Mr Møller's voice replied, even more softly. 'He'll have to know sooner or later.'

Mrs Møller said that was his affair; it was he, not she, who had taken on this job, and Mr Møller said: 'Oh well, let him sleep another half hour then; we can have our breakfast in peace.'

Their footsteps faded down the stairs.

Chris got completely dressed without noticing what he was doing. What would he have to know sooner or later? Had something happened to Father? Chris was always a little frightened, in his heart of hearts, when Father was flying. But yesterday he hadn't . . .?

If Father had crashed, if these Møllers had undertaken to tell him about it, they would not have talked about having their breakfast in peace . . . And Mother – Mother would never let strangers tell him about something terrible. But what if she had been sent for? Yes, but then there was Jørgen.

Chris stood in the middle of the floor, letting his imagination run riot. Then he pulled himself together. Whatever was going on would have to be got over with and you never made anything better by losing your head. How could he get washed, now that he was locked in? He wanted to go to the lavatory, too.

The door next to the window was not locked. Passing through something which looked like a boy's room, he reached the passage and went to the bathroom. It was a quick catlick, but he brushed his teeth and tidied up a bit before going downstairs. His knees felt peculiarly weak, but no one would have noticed anything the matter with him, he checked up in the glass in the hall, before opening the door and saying 'Good morning'.

'Good morning, Christopher,' said Mrs Møller kindly, and Mr Møller nodded. They were sitting at the table, eating. 'Come and have some breakfast. Are you hungry?'

'Not particularly,' said Chris, 'but I would like to know something about these friends of Father's you have been talking to. Is . . . is my father . . . has anything happened to my father?' He hoped they could not hear that his voice was trembling a little, after all.

Mrs Møller got up abruptly and looked angrily at her husband. 'No, nothing at all, Christopher. Your father and mother are alive and well, there's nothing whatever the matter with them, I promise you!'

Chris looked from one to the other. Then he caught sight of a morning paper on the window seat. There was nothing about Father on the front page. Chris was so relieved that he plumped down at once on the chair which was pulled out for him and said: 'Tea, please,' when Mrs Møller asked.

Mr Møller looked at him in some irritation. 'Don't you usually wash before eating?' Chris looked him straight in the eyes. 'I *have* washed,' he said politely. 'You forgot to lock the other door.'

That did it! Mrs Møller laughed so heartily that she had to put her cup down, and if he himself had not been beginning to get angry again he would have laughed too, at the sight of Mr Møller's face.

'Poor Mogens,' chuckled Mrs Møller, 'you've got a lot to learn before you'll be a success as a kidnapper.'

Chris stopped the egg spoon on its way to his mouth. '*What?*' he said, startled.

'Be quiet, Inger! There's nothing wrong with your father, Christopher, except that I hope he is busy thinking things over carefully!'

'My father always does that,' Chris interrupted, in a deliberately irritating drawl. 'But if you think he can dream up ransom money out of the ground, you had better think again.'

Mr Møller frowned angrily. 'Who said anything about money? We're not interested in your father's money. I suppose you've heard of something called NATO?'

Chris nodded and reached for the butter. It was obvious that Mr Møller found it extremely provoking that he continued to eat his breakfast, and he was fully determined to empty the bread basket, even if it choked him.

'Excellent. The moment your father withdraws Denmark from NATO, you will go home. Not before.'

There were limits to the things you could put a calm face on. Thunderstruck, Chris dropped his knife, exclaiming: 'You must be round the bend!'

'Nothing "round the bend" about caring about your country, Christopher!' said Mr Møller sternly. 'I, and

17

many with me, don't want Denmark to be used as a pawn in America's war game . . . without this damned alliance we wouldn't be threatened by anyone . . . no one would harm a small neutral country, why should they? It is this capitalist, war-mad society which is round the bend, as you call it, and someone must have the courage to act, if Denmark isn't to be ruined!'

'Oh yes, of course it takes a lot of courage to go round snatching other people's children,' drawled Chris, continuing to spread butter on his bread.

Møller's face turned white and Mrs Møller said: 'Now now, Christopher, there's no reason to be cheeky!'

He would like to know what she *would* consider a reason, thought Chris, without answering. Møller pulled himself together with an effort and said shortly: 'No one is asking you to understand these things. No one will do anything to you, so you needn't be afraid; it's going to be a little dull for you in the mornings while Rasmus is at school – that's our boy, he's about the same age as you – but you'll have to pass the time with a book. My wife will make sure you're comfortable, you have only to say if you get hungry before lunch. But you must stay upstairs, and it's no good making any plans to escape. I'm going to work now, but Torben will sit on the stairs until I come home and if you look out of the bathroom window you will see there are two men busy repairing an old car. They will go on being busy. It's half a mile to our nearest neighbour and the station is three-quarters of an hour's walk from here. And now, goodbye.'

Mrs Møller went out with him and when she came back Chris rose to his feet. 'Thanks for the breakfast,' he said briefly. She looked as if she would have liked to speak, but bit her lip and said nothing, until Chris was at the door. 'You'll be able to find a book in Rasmus's room,' was all she said.

Chris thanked her as shortly as before and went upstairs. When he was nearly at the top, Torben appeared from somewhere down below and sat himself down on the bottom stair but one. Chris pretended not to have noticed him.

He went into the room where he had spent the night and deliberately did not slam the door.

So *that* was what came of one's father being Prime Minister.

2

Chris sat down on the edge of his bed and tried to think, but he could not. It was not so much that he was hopping mad; it was rather that his whole head was filled with total astonishment. 'Crazy nuts,' he thought, over and over again, even saying it aloud to himself. It was quite impossible that adult people in Denmark could think of behaving in such a raving mad, hysterical way.

Nevertheless, they had.

'I shall make the bed,' he muttered. It was easier to think if you were doing something with your hands at the same time and besides, that woman was not going to have the chance of touching *his* bed, or anything else which was his. The thought gave him an idea. He dropped the pillow, went over to the passage door and silently eased the key out; then he put it in again on his own side and turned it. Now they would have to knock when they wanted him!

When he had made the bed he gave it a final, appreciative pat; if only Mother could see it – she always said he was incapable of making his own bed. It wasn't true, it was just that it was much more comfortable when she did it. Then he went through Rasmus' room to the bathroom to check up on Møller's remarks about the men. They were true enough: there was an old blue saloon car across the drive, the bonnet was open and two men were ready to busy themselves under it if anyone passed.

Not that the side road looked as if anyone ever drove along it, or even walked. You wouldn't have believed there could be such a desolate, dreary place, so close to Copenhagen. Perhaps it was pretty here in summertime? In any case, for people who were going to pinch other people's children and hide them, it was obviously practical to live somewhere where it would be difficult to find them.

Chris gave an enormous yawn and turned away from the window. It would be better to think about something else, something practical. Getting angry did no good.

He went back to his own room, sat down at the table by the window and rested his chin on his hand, after having a look to see if there were a pear tree or a wild vine or something like that growing on the wall under his windows. There was nothing. In any case, he was not particularly good at climbing, but he could have done it if necessary – those two down there by the car could not stay there all day and all night as well.

For a moment Chris wondered if it would be possible to tear up the sheets to climb down, as people did in books, but he gave it up as story-book nonsense. He had seen his mother tearing material up like that and it made a terrific row, one which Torben could not help hearing. And who knew what other window he might pass on the way down, or whether he would have to drop the last bit of the way and break his arms and legs?

No, it would be better to think of something cunning; he was better at that kind of thing, too. And it would be best for Father if he could get away and be at home again before the police had to look for him, he was sure of that.

What had they done at home the night before, when they got the letter? First they would have waited for some time, to see if he was just late from the Chess Club and it all turned out to be a silly practical joke. Then Mother would have begun to get worried . . . then Father would have rung up . . . well, whom would he have rung? The Minister of Justice, perhaps; he would certainly be the best one to talk to the police without the papers hearing anything about it – and then Jørgen. Perhaps he would have rung Jørgen first and Jørgen could easily ring up Kim and pretend he had thought Chris had gone home with Kim from the Club. No one would become suspicious, for Kim's father and mother knew quite well that Jørgen lived at the University and not at home.

Then they would have found out that he had been at the Club, just as usual, and had left, just as usual, at the normal time. What then?

Chris narrowed his eyes and followed the flight of two birds which were whirling through the air like stray notes of music in a cartoon film, against the dark grey sky outside.

Then they would have waited a little longer, but anything to do with NATO and the Middle East and that kind of thing had to be dealt with; otherwise there would be demonstrations and then they would have all that rubbish about the police 'being brutal and overturning prams' and the Treasury would have to supply the Embassies with new glass for their windows, and new railings.

Father said that there were many genuine idealists among the demonstrators and you should always try to understand their point of view, but you wouldn't feel much like doing that, when the Government might have been forced to hold an emergency meeting half the night and Hansen and the other chauffeurs, who would otherwise have had an early evening, had to be dragged out into the bad weather again – all because one schoolboy had been led by the nose!

Oh well, it was no use crying over that spilt milk; he could not think how he could have helped believing what Møller said. You did not go around expecting to be kidnapped, just because your Father happened to be Prime Minister. For the time being they would probably have agreed to let a little time pass – at least if Father had been left to decide – while the police quietly had a look round in the places where they might expect to find old nails and paving-stones and other missiles that demonstrators sometimes used. That would be all, if he himself could find a way of escaping in the meanwhile. There was no chance before dark; even if he could trick Torben into leaving the stairs and creep out and across the fields, the two men with the saloon car would see which way he went and as long as they were familiar with the place it would be as easy as anything for them to cut him off further away. If only it had been summer . . . But with all those big, bare fields everywhere, even a kitten would be discovered as soon as it moved.

What if he were to fall ill? They would have to call for a doctor and they would be discovered. How did you make yourself sick quickly? The medicine cupboard . . . perhaps there was something in the medicine cupboard.

Chris returned to the bathroom. There were a number of bottles and pills there; if only he knew the name of some medicines! It would be too bad if there was

22

something poisonous enough to make you fall down dead as a doornail, beyond hope of revival.

Codyl. He knew what that was: you used it for headaches and sore throats. Now, what if he were to take ten or twenty of those, or perhaps fifteen would be enough, and leave the pill bottle on the table and fall heavily to the floor as soon as he had taken them? Surely Codyl was not so poisonous that they would not be able to get hold of a doctor and pump him out in time? Chris did not care much for the plan, but something had to be done, and you didn't die of being pumped out, even if it was bound to be horribly uncomfortable.

He ran cold water into the tooth glass. Then he stopped. It would not do!

Father and Mother had never said anything about it, but he had been only ten years old when Father was elected Prime Minister, and Jørgen had said it, just once, a little later: 'You're not awfully old, Chris, so I think I might as well say this in case you don't think of it yourself. There are some people who will pay special attention to you now, teachers and other boys' parents, perhaps, because of Father. Try as hard as you can not to get yourself noticed! It would all come back on Dad, you see. Both of us will have to make sure that there is not too much about us to criticize, so that Dad's opponents can go round talking in pubs about him not even being able to bring up his own children properly!'

As a rule Jørgen was a frightful tease, of course, but when there was something he really wanted to tell you he always did it so calmly and carefully that you paid attention at once.

Chris knew what Jørgen had meant now. If he took all those pills and was unconscious before the doctor came, he could not tell the whole story and it would not be many days before someone began to spread rumours about him being a junky or a drug addict or something. There were always some people who preferred to think the worst.

Chris poured the water out again, put the bottle of pills back in its place and made for his room. When he reached Rasmus' room he stopped and looked around. What kind of a boy was Rasmus? The room was in rather a mess, but so was the whole house; some of the books were the right way up, some upside down, or lying flat – but he did have some of the books which Chris had himself. There was some Dickens, and something about Africa and help for the developing countries and a whole stack of manuals of technology, as well as one or two about animals and plants. School books, of course, and something about politics, and on top of a pile of tattered comics there was Sartre's Explanation of Existentialism.

Well, if Rasmus understood much of that he was too bright to talk to at all, thought Chris. But perhaps he played chess. There was no board lying about, or he could have played against himself; time passed so slowly and it would be an eternity before it was dark. If only he had had a transistor . . . there was one, by the bed!

Chris put the historical atlas on the table in his own room and turned on the radio. It was almost eleven o'clock and the music programme had a news bulletin every hour on the hour, so he would know almost at once if anything had been said.

Perhaps it would not be all that stupid to remain where he was until Father and Mother had to broadcast an SOS for him? There would certainly be a whole lot of ordinary, nice people who would be furious about it – people with children! And it could not possibly hurt Father.

Chris yawned again; all the same, he was going to take advantage of any opportunity to escape.

He had just heard the twelve o'clock bulletin when

someone turned the door handle. 'Open up, Christopher,' said Mrs Møller from outside. 'Here's your lunch.'

Chris opened the door and held it for her while she edged her way in with the tray. 'I don't know what you're used to eating, so I've made the kind of sandwiches I make for Rasmus. Tell me if you want any more. And you can have more milk. And stop locking that door, no one is going to harm you.'

'I prefer to lock it myself from inside before someone else does it from outside,' said Chris firmly.

Mrs Møller pushed the short, smooth fair hair back from her eyes. She was very pretty really, not the least bit fat, but she was sloppily dressed, and she looked tired, as if she were sick of all this. 'Your door won't be locked in the daytime,' she said, and added slowly, almost unwillingly: 'Christopher – try to take it as well as you can, all this. I can quite understand that you must think my husband is . . . that he's not very nice and is not treating you well. I would so much like you to believe that he doesn't mean any harm by it, but on the contrary, he thinks that something good can come of it, for the country. Rasmus is fond of his father and Tina almost worships him – she's Rasmus' little sister . . .'

'Is she at school too?' asked Chris. He preferred to talk about something other than Møller. After all, he was her husband.

Mrs Møller said that Tina was only four years old. 'She's over in . . . she's visiting a friend of mine, for the moment.'

It was all rather hard luck for Mrs Møller; yet this morning, when she started to laugh, she had looked quite normally bright and happy. Chris decided to have a go at making her understand.

'I can quite easily see that your husband hasn't anything particular against *me*, after all he doesn't know me at all

25

and it would be rather silly of a grown-up man to bother a thirteen-year-old boy he doesn't know. But, Mrs Møller, there's going to be the most awful fuss if Father and Mother have to announce publicly that I'm missing, and it's you and your husband who will suffer – and Rasmus. The little girl is so young. Couldn't you try to talk some sense into your husband? It's all the same to me if I miss a few days of school, as long as Father and Mother know where I am – or know I am all right, at least – but what about you? Don't you see that this is an absolutely feeble-minded plan? Father *can't* simply get up and withdraw the country from anything; he's the Prime Minister, not a dictator. He has to keep the law of the land, and it doesn't let you do that kind of thing! I can't understand why your husband doesn't know that,' Chris concluded irritably.

'He does know, Christopher, but he thinks he can force your father to have a referendum – you know what that is, don't you?'

'Yes, of course I know what a referendum is.' Chris shook his head helplessly. 'But – oh, I've forgotten again what you have to do – Father explained it to me once. I'm sure you only have to say you want it! If there are enough people who want a referendum, they have one – you don't have to go around stealing other people's children to get it, for crying out loud!'

'Well, that's what my husband thinks,' said Mrs Møller, pushing her hair back again.

There was no answer to that but 'Oh!'

Mrs Møller asked if he had found something to read and Chris said that was no trouble, but if she had finished with the morning paper he would like to read it.

Mrs Møller promised to bring it up and Chris began on his meal. There was some more of that good home-made bread – in fact it was more like Sunday lunch, with cress and chopped onions and radishes and cheese. And their liver sausage was marvellous.

Chris ate hungrily while he considered the situation. There was no doubt that Mrs Møller was unhappy about it. If only her husband would listen to her, because she didn't agree with him, Chris was sure of that. Well, she did agree about NATO, but not that it was a good idea to kidnap people.

He screwed up his eyes to concentrate, while he enjoyed the last bit of liver-sausage. If only he could explain to her what would happen to Rasmus at school if anyone got to know that his father had turned into a criminal; perhaps then she could be persuaded to let him go? But she had probably been trying to put Møller off the idea for some time. If there was anything about which Mother disagreed with Father, she would talk him to death all evening, and then, if he said: 'Now I've listened to everything you've said and you have not convinced me, so I shall have to do what *I* think best,' Mother always said: 'Yes, of course'. And she didn't protest any more, even if she continued to be critical. No, if the Møllers were old-fashioned as far as marriage was concerned and really cared about each other, there was nothing to be done. Mrs Møller could criticize as much as she liked, but she would not work against her own husband.

What was he to do? You could work out a lot about people when you saw what their homes looked like. He closed his eyes and thought of the rooms he had been in down below.

First the hall. A blue-green, tall chest of drawers, quite modern, with an oval mirror over it in a funny, ornamental gold frame. A kind of rush matting on the floor. Rubber boots, coats, a blue-painted chair with a rush seat – a real

27

one, not made of plastic. Gloves and oddments in a basket on the chest of drawers.

There were books in the living-room, not the kind of books some people have, which looked as if no one had read them, just standing in a neat row of bindings; there was a proper, long shelf with books of all different sizes and colours, and some pushed in on top of the others because there was no room. An old sofa and a red, modern one opposite each other, with a low table between them. A rocking-chair with coloured cushions, nice. A bureau, nice too, but there were one or perhaps two knobs missing from the drawers. A great mess of papers on the flap. A checked carpet on the floor, an old photograph in an old-fashioned frame on either side of the bureau. The rest of the pictures madly modern, so that you couldn't see if they represented anything; there was one of them which you noticed, so it was probably good.

No, he could see nothing which pointed to a particular profession. The Møllers were used to reading a lot, they were modern, but they also liked to have old things. Some of their things were dull, but they had nothing you could actually say was rubbish. Mrs Møller was slovenly, you could see that from the ashtray, which was emptied, but not wiped round afterwards. Perhaps she was just busy, after all? Because when she had laid the table for dinner, it looked nice and inviting, with flowers and clean napkins, and hot plates and everything . . .

Chris resigned himself to the fact that the Møllers were perfectly ordinary people, like anyone else one knew, nothing to get hold of, nothing which told you what they did, or who they were. If they took him down to the living-room for dinner that evening, he must have a look at the books they read. You could always tell something from what people read. Perhaps they weren't even called Møller?

He could not remember seeing a name on the door the night before, but it probably was their name. Lying about your name did not really match up with laying the table properly and having a houseful of books. And as long as he had no idea where they lived, it did not really matter his knowing their name, since it was a very common one.

Yes, but there was one thing which he did know, Chris thought, brightening suddenly. He had looked at his compass many times as they travelled and he was quite certain that they were west of Copenhagen and not in North Zealand. And they didn't know that he knew!

Perhaps Rasmus had a map of the Copenhagen area . . . but first there was the one o'clock news.

Nobody said anything about a kidnapping. On the other hand, Rasmus *did* have a map – and better than that, he had a train timetable and a bus timetable, and in them, cripes, yes! There was his address, as clear as day! The house they lived in was called 'The Forge' and the address was Reerslev. And the connections to Copenhagen were underlined in red. Good Lord, what a lot of thickheads!

But Chris's enthusiasm quickly faded. As long as he was guarded like a dangerous criminal, inside the house, it was of no practical importance that he knew where he was and how to get to Copenhagen. Nonetheless, he replaced the map and the timetables carefully where he had found them; you never knew . . .

Then he took off his watch and put it in his trouser pocket. No one had seen it yet, but Rasmus was sure to notice if he kept it on. It was quite a special watch. He was not supposed to have it until he was confirmed, but when his old school watch stopped, Father and Mother said it was too silly to buy another cheap one. If Rasmus

29

knew anything about existentialism, he would not be too stupid to notice the compass. And the others had the upper hand, for the time being. There was no need to give away the miserable little advantage he had.

Someone heavy was coming up the stairs. Chris just managed to sit down and look out of the window before the man called Torben came bursting in. 'The morning paper, Your Excellency,' he said. 'We can't have you not knowing the Stock Exchange rates, can we?'

Chris did not answer. There was no reason why he should reply to such rubbish. The young man reached one sweatered arm over his shoulder and switched on the transistor on medium wave. A German voice bellowed across the room.

'Do you know German?'

'Very little,' said Chris shortly, feeling suddenly quite stiff inside with fury: what a boor!

Torben flung himself into a chair, making it creak, and Chris opened the newspaper. No one could expect him to be too well-behaved with a . . . a creature like that! He let the voice go on bellowing for a time and then said politely: 'Would you please turn the radio down a bit? I can't read with all that row.'

The young man switched it right off. 'I forget you couldn't understand German. Why do you talk in that silly way? We don't have any bourgeois behaviour here.'

'If bourgeois means polite, I agree with you!' Chris snapped.

'One in the eye for me, eh?' Torben grinned. 'Well, what the hell, I don't blame you for being as mad as a coot, you maladjusted little creep!'

It actually sounded quite friendly, but Chris couldn't bear being called a creep.

Well, he had tried to be friendly and make an effort to chat about something, and he was plainly not stupid,
30

thought Chris, when Torben had gone down again. But he didn't have any particular desire to talk to people who were acting as his prison warder. He had answered as shortly as he possibly could and in the end Torben had said: 'Oh well, if you don't intend to open your mouth, you don't. If you get any different ideas, you can call. It's not all that bloody funny sitting staring at the stairs all day long.'

Chris had said: 'Don't sit there then!' And Torben had grinned and said: 'Yes, you'd like that, wouldn't you?'

Perhaps it was stupid of him, not wanting to talk to them? Perhaps, if he did talk to them, he might find out what made them have so many hysterical and unpractical ideas. But it made him so furious every time he remembered that they had quite calmly locked him in.

Besides, Torben could not open his mouth without 'devil' and 'hell' and 'bloody' flying round your ears, and he just wasn't used to it.

How sleepy he was . . . and it would be a long time before Rasmus got home from school. Chris lay down on the bed and a moment later he was asleep.

He woke up again a little before three and switched on the radio.

'. . . the Foreign Minister should have been speaking at a meeting in Kolding this evening, but had to cancel it, owing to a severe cold . . .'

It *might* be true, of course, people *did* get colds sometimes; but it might also be an excuse. From time to time, when you wanted to hold a Cabinet meeting without the newspapers getting hold of it, you had to use an excuse like that, if there was someone who would not have been able to come otherwise.

And there would be all the people who had hired a hall and ordered lots of coffee and cakes for afterwards – and the people who had arranged babysitters so that they could go – and now the Foreign Minister would have to find another day for that particular meeting, as they had all done so much hard work . . .

Crikey, how embarrassing, if it was because of him!

Someone came thundering up the stairs, past his door – 'Ah, there you are! Hi . . . what the hell, you've got long hair!'

3

He actually found himself laughing: Rasmus looked almost as if he had fallen from the moon. But there was not much point in laughing if you had no one to laugh with, and Rasmus was just standing in the doorway, scowling and looking more and more annoyed.

'Why shouldn't I have long hair? You've got long hair yourself,' said Chris pleasantly. 'One is more or less forced to . . .'

Rasmus repeated 'forced to?' as if it were a foreign expression he had never come across before.

'Yes, forced to . . . at least in my class. Only three boys have an old-fashioned hair-cut and they hear about it on every possible occasion. They haven't even got it because they want to, it's just because their parents want them to.'

'Does your father *let* you?' asked Rasmus incredulously. 'Have long hair, I mean?'

'Yes, of course he lets me!' It wasn't really a lie, because although Father most certainly teased him about it and scolded a bit when Mother said it was really too much, neither of them would have said a word about it if they had known he only let it grow to avoid giving the other boys ammunition against his father.

'Well!' said Rasmus, looking quite amazed. He was tall, with broad shoulders, and very nice looking, in a way. He had the same bright blue eyes as his mother. But it must have been at least a week since he had washed his hair . . . Perhaps he couldn't do anything else but look staggered? Well, they must talk about something. Chris said he only wished it was not so impractical always having to wash the stuff, and Rasmus looked scornful for a change and suggested that he might simply stop washing it.

Chris pretended not to have noticed the scorn. 'Yes, but I can't do that,' he explained peaceably. 'If it gets greasy and flops over my glasses I can neither hear nor see. In any case, it's uncomfortable for oneself and everyone else if it looks like heaven knows what and smells mucky. In fact, I wish it would become trendy to decide for yourself, without anyone interfering.'

His relief at having another boy to talk to drained away as the afternoon passed. Rasmus was maddening. Chris thought it must have been feeling so much at a loss which had made him forget that it was only adults who thought that as long as children were the same age, everything would be all right.

Even a maddening chap was better than no one at all, and if one tried long enough there must surely be *something* they could do together, or even talk naturally about. But Rasmus was suspicious all the time.

It was strange. People you didn't know were like that sometimes, of course, if their father and mother had gone on and on about one's father being the Prime Minister, but that usually disappeared in time, and in any case,

Rasmus' father was not silly and impressed . . . on the contrary! thought Chris. It would have been some use if he *had* been impressed enough not to go and kidnap one like a piglet in a sack.

They were given fruit juice and sandwiches and apples. Rasmus fetched it but when they had eaten, things began to go wrong – as if it were not perfectly reasonable to clear away, so that everything could be included in the washing-up!

'You can shift the crocks yourself,' Rasmus bellowed over the sound of a pop record blasting from the radio. 'I'm damned if I'm going to be your waiter, you scum!'

Chris thrust his hands deep into his pockets. 'Well, I wouldn't at all mind going down with it myself, if you can get Torben off the stairs,' he said calmly. 'Your mother will want the things for the washing-up, won't she?'

Rasmus found plenty more to grouse about: now it was also wrong for Mrs Møller to have to wash up after 'someone like you'; but in the end he took the tray down, when Chris did not answer.

He was away for some time and Chris took his hands out of his pockets. He must watch out and not get angry. Rasmus must not succeed in irritating him, because they would simply end up by coming to blows, and things were bad enough already for Mrs Møller, without one's fighting her stupid son into the bargain. Being stupid was something he couldn't help and one would have to make oneself grin inwardly when he was being particularly illogical, instead of being irritated.

Rasmus brought some more apples with him when he came up again and put them down on the table beside the radio. With a bit of goodwill you could see that as an apology.

'Don't you think we could try to keep the peace?' said Chris politely. 'You don't have to entertain me if you don't want to – it's neither your fault nor mine that I'm here. But I think it's quite idiotic for us to quarrel before we actually know each other at all.'

Rasmus mumbled something about it's not being he who was quarrelling and bit into an apple. 'Eat up,' he said, 'we've got masses and masses.'

'And they're good, too,' said Chris. So there was something they could agree about.

Then he had the bright idea that they could do Rasmus' homework for tomorrow. They spent an hour and a half on that, because Rasmus had preparation to do for the maths lesson and he was as thick as two planks about it. When Chris discovered this he was tempted for a moment simply to work the whole lot out for him at high speed; but for one thing, if he did that he would, quite honestly, be showing off; and if he could manage to explain the problems a bit more time would pass without their quarrelling.

Actually, Rasmus wasn't really stupid; as long as one was talking about something definite, nothing to do with opinions or people, he could use his head quite well.

'Well, boys, how are you getting on? Good Lord, are you doing homework?' It was Møller who had just put his head in at the door.

'Hello,' said Rasmus casually. 'He's a real swot!'

Chris said he was only good at maths. 'I'm no good at languages, for instance.'

'They're as easy as pie,' exclaimed Rasmus scornfully, and Møller said that it must be the teacher's fault.

Chris shook his head. 'No, it's not the grammar, that's logical enough, or even the exceptions, because you only have to learn them, like a vocabulary. But I've got no ear for languages, you see, and the teacher can't do anything about that.'

35

Møller brought the subject round to schools in general and Chris sighed inwardly. If only he would go away!

Møller asked how the Pupils' Council worked at Chris's school and Chris could not suppress a wry grin. 'At our school it's more or less a matter of form,' he said. 'Our teachers have always been easy to talk to, most of them are nice, so if we have a sensible explanation for something we want, they have always agreed to try it.'

'But you must *use* your Pupils' Council,' said Møller solemnly. 'Not all schools are as good as that, and the Pupils' Council must protect the children against injustice. It's your *right* to use it.'

'Perhaps you'd rather do away with it altogether!'

If only that impossible boy could say something without sounding as if he would prefer to finish every sentence with 'you stupid pig'.

'Oh no, it's quite practical,' said Chris peaceably, 'meeting at fixed times, I mean, and being able to talk about things and write down what you can agree on. It saves time for both sides and you don't go on brooding over things until you get angry about them. It's just that I can't see that it matters, if you're in a situation when you can talk to your teachers in any case.'

Rasmus sniffed disparagingly. 'I suppose you're trying to tell me that the teachers are quite prepared to let you smoke or go out, and to give up writing reports?'

'But why should they? Why should you have the right to do what you like? Grown-ups can't do that either. For instance, if you were having an operation I certainly don't think you would like it if the doctor was blowing smoke in your face, or suddenly took it into his head to go shopping before sewing you up again! And reports can sometimes be useful . . . some parents haven't got time to go to Parents' Meetings, or they may be too embarrassed, and then how are they to find out what their children are up to and what they should be helping them with? But as far as I'm concerned you can throw the report book out of the window, if you like. I just think it's very stupid of you to be so set on making us the enemies of the teachers. Most of them became teachers because they thought it would be interesting to take a bunch of kids who didn't know anything about anything and make sure they know something about everything, by the time they finished school. Teachers aren't our enemies, are they? Or are you trying to tell me that all schoolchildren are angels and so bright that they know more about school than the teachers?'

'You don't understand a shit about it,' shouted Rasmus angrily. 'It's . . .'

'There, there,' his father interrupted. 'Take it easy, now! Rasmus is not very keen on authority, Chris, and we've brought him up to believe that children have the same rights as adults.'

'Oh!' said Chris, because he couldn't think of any other answer to such a stupid remark.

'. . . but you are not like that, of course,' sneered Rasmus.

Chris yawned. 'No, I'm not,' he drawled. 'My parents know perfectly well that I don't know enough to decide everything for myself yet, so they do it for me. If I was allowed to decide on my own bedtime, for instance, I would be two hours late for school every morning. But I think we ought to stop discussing our parents, because I've noticed you don't at all like being contradicted.'

'What do you say, Ras? Is there any truth in it?' said Møller. Chris got up and excused himself – he was just going to the lavatory. It would be just like Møller not to know that you don't tick your son off when other children are listening.

It was too dark now to see if the two men were still

37

busy with the car. If he ran the other way they would not be able to see him in the darkness, either, even if they were there. The problem was to get out of the house. If they brought his food up, there was nothing he could do. If he came down and ate with the others, it would be a question of keeping his wits about him and seizing the opportunity. The doors would be locked – they weren't as stupid as all that. Then there were the windows. Chris narrowed his eyes and saw them in front of him: they were the type with small panes, with wood between them. In a thriller you smashed a pane, but what did you do in reality? If only they had been one sheet of glass, and if you had the time, of course, you would use a cushion or something to break it, so that you didn't cut your wrists and get nowhere anyway. But very small panes with wood in between were too strong for you to be able to break both at once.

Perhaps, if he could start helping to carry the washing-up out without their thinking about it – if he could manage it so that he was alone in the kitchen, even for a moment, he would be able to open a window and jump out. That is, if the windows didn't stick. If they had to be banged open, the alarm would be given too soon, and he must have a bit of a start.

There were too many ifs about it, thought Chris drearily. The police must be searching for him flat out by now, but that could take time. There had been no one around on the road the night before, when Møller fooled him, so they would have to go through the files and begin at one end with all the activists. Would they be listed, in any case? Well, the ones who had been sentenced for causing violent disturbances would have to be listed somewhere. That Torben looked as if he might easily throw paving-stones about, from the way he came barging in and gave orders. But if he didn't live here, if he was

38

only here to play prison guard, they would not be able to find him.

And neither Møller himself nor Mrs Møller looked as if they would be very good at rioting; if they were the kind of people who went home when the proper demonstration was over, before the hooliganism began . . . there was no knowing how long it would take to trace them.

Meanwhile, he would have to sit like a battery-calf, moping half the day and quarrelling with Rasmus the other half!

Well, but now at least Møller must have finished ticking Rasmus off – not that he had sounded angry, actually, but whatever he thought about politics and so on – he couldn't avoid hearing how Rasmus had snarled and sneered.

Chris opened the door to Rasmus' room soundlessly and waited a moment to make sure that the ticking off was over. Then he stayed where he was a little longer – Rasmus was not being scolded at all, they were talking quite normally, and they were talking about him; that was what came of listening at doors! Chris narrowed his eyes. If he was to have a chance of escaping, he could not worry too much about principles of that kind; in the end it would even be to their own advantage if he could fool them – though they would be too stupid to see it. They weren't actually stupid of course; fanatical was what Father called it – too intense to give a hang for sense and logic.

'. . . but he's so damned wet, Dad . . . He's good at maths, but otherwise . . .'

'You must remember that he has had a bourgeois upbringing, Ras; I'm not at all sure that he is as wet as you think. Aren't you becoming rather over-picturesque in your language, by the way? It sounds pretty extreme beside Chris's, it seems to me.'

Inevitably, Rasmus at once exploded with 'Perhaps you'd like to change sons?' but Møller's voice only sounded rather tired: 'That's a load of damned rubbish, my lad, and well you know it! Chris has been brought up in the midst of a basically rotten society and not educated to think for himself, so naturally he apes what he hears at home. That doesn't mean that there's anything wrong with him, all the same. In fact, I think he handles the situation extremely well, for such a bourgeois brat.'

Rasmus again, but in a quite different voice, almost tearfully: 'It's all his damned fault – Mum, and Tina and everything.'

Oh no, this was too uncomfortable for words! If only they had said something practical which he could use, but standing here spying on private things – ! Chris pushed the door open and closed it behind him and Rasmus and his father quickly talked about something else. When Chris came into the next room Møller got to his feet and said that they would be eating in half an hour.

'Bring Chris down with you, Ras, we can keep an eye on him now, and it's too gloomy for him sitting up here alone.' He smiled kindly and went off, his head bowed.

Rasmus stood with his back turned and switched the radio from one station to another. Chris remembered how his voice had sounded and made a quick decision.

'Switch the box off, Rasmus, and tell me something: just as I was coming in now I heard you say something about there being something wrong with your mother and little sister. If you've got something you want to talk about which will be difficult if I come down with you, I'll just stay up here – you've only to say.'

Rasmus turned abruptly. 'We've got absolutely nothing to talk about and it's all your fault,' he said furiously.

'Mine!' Chris put astonishment into his voice. 'Now look here, Rasmus, I've never so much as seen your little
40

sister, and as for your mother, I certainly haven't gone out of my way to be well-behaved, you can hardly expect that, if you use your bad-tempered skull to think with! But I *have* talked politely to her, the few times we've talked at all.'

Rasmus sat down, his head bowed forward a little, like his father. 'Mum and Dad are angry with each other. Mum's angry because Dad agreed to – to use you as a weapon. And Dad's angry because she's taken her revenge by sending Tina away. And it's all your fault.' He no longer sounded furious, but almost as if he were trying to convince himself of something.

Chris looked at him anxiously. So it wasn't so strange, after all, that Rasmus was always attacking him.

'But Rasmus, that must be nonsense, mustn't it? After all, it's not because of me, it's because your father and my father have different ideas about politics. I don't think we ought to talk about that, because we'll only have a row and it's got nothing to do with us what our fathers think. But your mother can't possibly have revenged herself on your father . . . she wouldn't do a thing like that.'

'She told him I was old enough to think for myself, but she wasn't going to have a criminal as a father for a . . . for Tina, who's only four years old. So she drove her over to stay with Gerda.'

And now, if Chris were to say that Mrs Møller was absolutely right, there would be a fight, because you simply couldn't say that about someone's father! It was tough luck for Rasmus to have his father and mother fighting.

'Oh, but it was only because she was angry,' he said quickly. 'Think about it, man! They will soon make friends again, if they usually get on well. And if the police can find me quickly, so that your father doesn't have to go to prison.'

'Mother's all right, actually,' said Rasmus. 'It's just that mothers are too soft. You have to be prepared to make sacrifices.'

'Yes, so your mother doesn't think your little sister should have to make sacrifices, since she's too small to understand anything about it.'

'Tina isn't damn well sacrificing a shit, Gerda spoils her to hell when she's there,' Rasmus burst out.

Chris gave him a grave look. 'But when she's bigger, she would probably prefer to have a father who had not done anything he could go to prison for.'

'I suppose you think *I'm* dead keen to have my father put inside?' Rasmus began to tramp up and down the floor. 'Why can't *your* father just do as he's asked? Perhaps he doesn't care about *you*?'

'Yes, he does,' said Chris seriously. 'But he cares about doing his work so that people can rely on him, as well. And they wouldn't be able to, if one man could force him to do something just because of something private about *me*. So he has to put up with not knowing where I am and just hope that no one is doing anything to me.'

Rasmus came over and stood immediately in front of him, so that it was quite obvious that he was the taller. 'I shouldn't be so bloody sure about that if I was you!' he said viciously.

Chris clenched his hands in his pockets. Don't be drawn . . . don't use the only real weapon you've got at the wrong moment, just because you're angry.

'Oh, take a running jump! I'm sorry you've got your own troubles, but it's no fault of mine, and if you can't think of anything better than crazy threats, we might as well go down.'

Torben went into the living-room with them when they

came downstairs. Møller was looking out of the window into the darkness, the table was laid and they could hear Mrs Møller out in the kitchen. Torben moved across in front of Møller and drew the curtains; there was no need to tempt curious passers-by, he said. Møller shrugged his shoulders and said there wouldn't be any damn' fools wandering round a ploughed field in the dark in mid-November; but he allowed the curtains to be drawn.

Chris quickly turned his eyes away from the telephone standing on the bookcase, but not quickly enough. 'And we'd better watch out that he doesn't get too temptingly close to the telephone,' said Torben. 'In case he gets seized with an urge to ring home to his mothah!'

Møller got up, pulled out the plug and took the telephone upstairs. When he came down again, he said: 'As long as Chris is in this house, you can treat him properly, and that goes for the others, too. He hasn't shown the slightest sign of being a cry-baby, and it's not *him* we have a quarrel with.'

Torben said 'Oh, God forbid!' but he looked studiedly careless, the way people do when they feel foolish, and a moment later he went out to the kitchen.

Rasmus had flung himself down in a chair, but when Mr Møller looked over the top of his newspaper and said he might like tc go out and see if there was anything he could do to help his mother, he too vanished.

Mr Møller went on reading; now there really was an opportunity to go and look at the books and try to discover something, but Chris had suddenly lost the inclination. If only he could get away from here, he would be delighted to know nothing at all about Rasmus' parents.

He thought for a time and then said: 'What is it you have against my father? Apart from the NATO thing,

43

that is, because that wasn't something my father invented.'

Mr Møller laid his newspaper aside. 'I've got nothing against your father, as you know him, Chris. I've only talked to him once or twice. I'm sure he's a nice man, and a good father. I *have* got something against the way he wants the country to be governed, if you understand what I mean.'

Chris thought hard. 'Say it briefly!' his father always said, but that was what was so difficult. If only he could convince Mr Møller now.

'Yes, I understand that, naturally, but why don't you just *say* it? I simply can't understand why you think you'll get anywhere by locking me up and making my father and mother anxious. What would *you* say, if someone took Rasmus and locked him up, and you didn't know where he was?'

Mr Møller said that, of course, Chris didn't understand politics. 'From time to time, when something is very important to everybody, you have to cut through all the endless talk and get to the main point.'

'But if you cut through the talk, you're throwing the main point away, aren't you? Because if people don't want to talk things over any more, I don't think it's politics; it's simply using force to get your own way.'

Chris waited a little, but when Mr Møller did not reply at once, he added: 'In any case, it won't do any good – kidnapping me, I mean. You can lock me up for a month and nothing will happen, except that I miss school. You can never force my father to do anything if he thinks it's wrong.'

'We shall have to see, Chris,' was all Mr Møller said. 'But here's our meal coming in.' He smiled pleasantly and got up.

Chris sighed inwardly. But of course it was too much

44

to hope that he could convince a man who was quite certain that he was in the right, when he was only thirteen years old, and to be honest, not particularly thrilled about politics.

Mrs Møller nodded to him as they sat down, and while Mr Møller and Torben talked about someone who would be coming that evening, Chris tried to keep an eye on her. It was certainly true that she and Mr Møller were not on good terms. They spoke to each other calmly enough, but only about the vegetables and Rasmus' wellingtons and domestic matters like that, and they didn't really look at each other when they spoke. To Torben she scarcely spoke at all.

Rasmus, on the other hand, did. He must be keen on football, he went on and on talking about a match his club had played. Chris did his best not to listen, it wasn't easy to listen to Rasmus calmly.

'. . . and would you believe it, he loused up the bloody free kick, the arsehole . . .'

Chris put down his knife and fork.

'Aren't you hungry, Christopher?' asked Mrs Møller.

'Well . . .'

'Perhaps our food isn't good enough?' said Rasmus belligerently.

Suddenly Chris felt he had had enough.

'Oh yes, it is,' he said, looking straight at Rasmus. 'Your mother is a smashing cook. But I lose my appetite when you go on talking about bladders and bowels!'

Rasmus looked astounded, but Mrs Møller said pleasantly: 'I certainly see Christopher's point. I'm always asking Rasmus if we couldn't do without the lavatory in the living-room all day long, but nobody listens to what I say in this house . . .'

'It's got bloody nothing to do with that!'

Chris almost grinned. Rasmus had begun in a great

45

rage, and then the last part of the sentence came out much more slowly, as he began to think. 'What the hell are you supposed to say?' he finished irritably.

Chris said you could use swear words which didn't mean anything in themselves.

'What sort of words?'

'Oh . . . like hang and blow and darn and blazes, for instance.'

Torben pointed a fork at him: 'Allow me to inform you that "darn" is simply a way of not saying damn, and "blazes" is a popular version of hell!'

'Yes, I know that,' said Chris shortly, 'but the words don't really mean anything any more, because no one really thinks that there is such a thing as damnation or an actual place called hell. But there's no doubt about the results of your digestive system. In any case, it's more fun inventing words for yourself.'

Rasmus and the adults all began to talk at once, and Chris became absorbed in his own thoughts. He wanted to get home; he had not been able to pass on his word from the night before: 'miasmal'. He had been quite proud of that. What had his mother thought of, he wondered? She was the one who had started it all. One day she had said that she was gradually forgetting to listen to what they said in Parliament, because she was always counting up how many times the members said 'at this point in time' and 'situation-wise' and 'with respect', and so on.

His father had asked in alarm if he said things like that too, and he did, because it was catching! So he had agreed that all three of them should have a new word for him every evening. Jørgen sometimes found the craziest words, but they were all written down, and Father actually used some of them from time to time – in any case it was good fun.

Chris swallowed a yawn, because that Torben was not going to have the satisfaction of seeing that he was feeling low. Of course, none of *them* knew that he always started yawning when there was anything wrong . . .

There was a television in the corner. They would probably watch the television news . . . Would anything be said? It was two hours since he had heard the time pips. Rasmus' voice penetrated his thoughts: '. . . Christopher says "cripes".'

So at least he sometimes hears what I'm saying, thought Chris.

They were apparently all busy making up swear-words; Rasmus was laughing – he looked quite nice when he laughed – and Chris noticed Mr and Mrs Møller smiling at each other, not deliberately, because their faces took on a grudging expression immediately afterwards – but as if it was something they normally did.

Well, yes, there was that business about the little sister. 'Mrs Møller . . .'

'Yes, Christopher? What are you dreaming about?'

Well, one might as well just say it straight out! 'About Rasmus' little sister – of course *you* know where she is, but I was thinking – if you have sent her away because of me, you might just as well get her back again. I mean, I won't say anything when she's listening. And since she's so little, she won't see anything odd in someone sitting on the stairs all day long, a prison guard, I mean . . .'

The silence round the table was so heavy that he wished he had not said anything. He might just as well have left it – only it was hard luck on Rasmus, the silly clot. Parents ought not to mix their children up in grown-up affairs, which they couldn't do anything about.

'That's very nice of you, Chris,' Mr Møller said at last. 'But I'm sure my wife thinks . . .'

Mrs Møller interrupted him: 'I don't think anything,

47

Mogens. Christopher is not one to make idle promises; I already know him well enough to be sure of that. So if you could manage to pick her up tomorrow, before you go . . . before you have to go to work . . .'

Rasmus began to try to stare him down. Chris stared back, and in the end Rasmus smiled a wry little smile before looking away.

That was that. Now, perhaps, he would be a little easier to get on with.

4

They had just finished eating when the doorbell rang. Mr Møller went out and opened the door. There was obviously more than one person – if they were unexpected guests, then . . . But Chris got no further in his plans, because he could hear that, on the contrary, the visitors were expected. Mrs Møller put her head out into the hall and said that they should 'go into Mogens' room for a bit'. The door to a room on one side stood open, this was obviously Mr Møller's room. 'Hell, are you still shovelling it into you?' said one man from inside the room. 'We *have* eaten, Inger, so you needn't worry about your rissoles!'

Mr Møller came back from the other room. He turned his head at the door and said they needn't worry, there would be a rissole left for supper. He was smiling, but all the furrows in his face looked as if the smile creaked.

'It would be reasonable to let the **boy** watch the TV

news before he is sent up to bed, don't you think?' said Mrs Møller aloud. 'We're not waging a war of nerves against children, and you so generously agreed that Mogens and I should be the only people the boy would have a chance of recognizing . . .'

Somebody said calmly from inside the room that it was impractical to risk winding up the whole group, and Mr Møller said 'Of course', and that he would turn up the sound. He stroked Mrs Møller's hair, as if by chance, when he passed her on the way to the television.

There was nothing in the headlines and Torben said, in surprise: 'Do you think they're shameless enough not to lift a finger, the pigs?'

Chris swallowed back a yawn and thought, clenching his teeth, that he jolly well hoped so. It was not until the home news that it came: 'Yesterday evening, activists kidnapped Prime Minister Egstrup's thirteen-year-old son in an attempt to force Denmark out of NATO. The Prime Minister received a letter at his home in the evening, stating that his son would be held until the Prime Minister declared from the Chair of the House Denmark's immediate withdrawal from NATO. The boy was expected home from a sports club at about ten p.m. but had failed to arrive. The police have no clues. We will bring you a statement by the Prime Minister in a few moments.'

Mr Møller had risen to his feet. Chris could see him from the side in the half-darkness. He had opened his mouth but not a sound came out, his Adam's apple wobbled up and down a few times, looking quite ridiculous, while the newsreader went on talking about a fire in the North. It was like watching a ventriloquist. At last he spoke:

'Is it too much to ask what happened to the letter we

49

agreed on, where we demanded a referendum on the subject?' he said. His voice sounded quite different.

Everyone began talking at once from the other room so that it was impossible to hear what they were saying – except that – yes – there was a woman with them!

'Sshhh, here comes His Excellency.'

Father looked perfectly normal on the screen, just as he always did. In fact, it was the interviewer who seemed rather nervous.

'You seem to be taking it quite calmly, Prime Minister?'

Father smiled pleasantly and said that he certainly was and Chris almost shouted 'Ha ha!' aloud.

'. . . and in fact it is not quite accurate to say that the police have no clues, because I have not asked the police for help. I thought the young people should be given a chance to send my son home tomorrow without any fuss.'

'So you have no intention of withdrawing Denmark from NATO, Prime Minister?'

'You know as well as I do that I am quite unable to do that.' That was how Father always sounded when someone asked a really silly question – friendly but rather patient. 'Let's keep our feet on the ground, shall we? You will see, when the young people – no names, people very seldom put their names to that type of letter – when they have had a chance to take a look at the laws by which the country is governed, they will no doubt manage to give the boy a ticket for the Underground, if he hasn't any money on him. And I shall think no worse of them for it.'

'But your son? Don't you think he's frightened?'

Father shifted a little in his chair and Chris stared fixedly at his right temple.

'Oh no, I don't think so. The young people write that they *tricked* him into coming, not that they knocked him down. And Christopher is calm by nature. He is sure to be pretty annoyed at what he will regard as a silly game, but otherwise, as long as there's a chess board around, he will get by. He will have to miss a few days of school, but he would have to do that if he caught a cold.'

'And if your son does not come home tomorrow?'

Father rose to his feet and smiled his that's-enough-of-that smile. 'Well, then of course we shall have to ask the police to go and fetch him.'

Then the letter appeared on the screen, magnified so that you could read it, but Chris paid no attention. All the others, including the ones from Mr Møller's room, went closer. This was his chance, in the semi-darkness!

But no. Torben, the wretch, had been keeping an eye on him after all. He was standing, leaning against the door, before Chris had done more than turn his head towards it. So that was no good. Perhaps there would be another opportunity, or perhaps they would work out from what the interviewer was reading from the Constitution that they might as well drive him home now.

Chris did not discover what they had agreed, because just then Mrs Møller said that he and Rasmus must go up. 'Not me, damn it, Mum!' Rasmus protested quite angrily, but Mr Møller turned and said: 'Yes. Up you go, both of you. *Now*, Rasmus!'

'Come on, Rasmus.' Chris pulled him along, not that he would not have loved to stay downstairs himself and hear how it ended, but Mr Møller had quite enough to cope with and it was silly to have themselves put out by force.

In any case, there was something very reassuring about a perfectly normal paternal order like that, in the midst of all this confusion.

Both of them went in through Chris's door, but without speaking to each other, and Rasmus went on to his own room at once.

Chris sat down and thought. It was great to have seen

51

Dad. Chris had been quite prepared to believe that nothing had happened to him, since Mrs Møller had said so, but it had been great all the same. One somehow didn't feel quite so far from home now, and it was obvious that Father wanted him to keep calm and not worry about school or anything.

But what was also obvious was that Dad was simply furious! People sometimes thought that they could play games with Dad, just because he didn't make a row or speak viciously of his opponents, as so many did. You couldn't see when he was angry, either, because he had had so much practice at not yawning, so you had to know him extremely well to know that when he was suppressing rage there was a little vein which throbbed in his right temple. And it had positively jumped when the interviewer asked if he thought Chris was frightened.

Rasmus was messing about with something in his room. Then he came to the door: 'I'm going down again now,' he said.

'Don't you think that Torben will be on guard?'

'I should think I've got a right to go where I like in my own house!' Rasmus looked angrily at him and Chris said: 'No contest, as far as I'm concerned. I'm not the one who's playing prison guards. And if you can find out if I'm to go home tonight or first thing in the morning, I should actually be quite interested to know.'

Rasmus gave him a scornful glance. 'You're the dullest damn zombie . . .'

Well well, that was a bit of an improvement anyway, thought Chris with a little grin.

He waited a bit and then got up. What if the road were actually clear and he could go down the stairs and straight out of the door . . .

Rasmus was standing down there with his eye to the keyhole and Chris went back to his room. Of course he could have knocked Rasmus out, but whether he could get even a few minutes' start outside the door was doubtful. In any case it would be a bit rough for Rasmus to be the one who was blamed, when it was the grownups who were idiots. And if they drove him home soon by themselves, or the police found him tomorrow or the day after, he would be able to avoid talking about the Møllers. They were rather nice, really, even if they had a few screws loose.

'They all keep shouting at once, you can't understand a word,' said Rasmus indignantly, sitting down on Chris's bed. Chris made a vague reply and asked if Rasmus had some game or other which they could play, which of course made Rasmus flare up again: hadn't he anything better than games in his nut and couldn't he see that there were more sensible things to do at a time like this?

Chris stuck his hands deep in his pockets. It wasn't any use saying that he knew Rasmus was furious with the others, who had been making a fool of his father.

'No, I really can't see that,' he said peaceably. 'There's nothing we *can* do, is there? We're not even allowed to be down there to hear what they're rowing about. I know you're upset, but if we talk about it you'll only get worse. So I thought we might as well do something we won't row about.'

It had not been exactly pleasant, though, thought Chris when they were both in bed in their own rooms a couple of hours later. Not because Rasmus was really stupid, but he had not the patience to understand an explanation; he scarcely listened at first and got in a temper later, when he lost. Chess had been completely hopeless and it had been really difficult to avoid beating him the whole time. They had actually finished up playing Ludo!

At nine o'clock Mrs Møller had called up the stairs that Rasmus could come down and fetch some tea and

53

sandwiches for them. That had been almost the most peaceful part of the evening, because Chris had asked where they bought that marvellous brown bread and it turned out that Mrs Møller baked it herself. And no one objected to others noticing that one's mother was pretty clever.

But Mrs Møller did not want to talk about what was happening downstairs. She had come up to fetch the tray, but when Rasmus asked she only said wearily that they must stop plaguing the life out of her, it was difficult enough already. And they could go to bed when they liked, because Chris would not be going home that night in any case.

He was hardly disappointed, because he had not believed in it either . . . not really.

When Rasmus had fallen asleep he had made an attempt to find the telephone which Mr Møller had taken upstairs before supper. Or rather, he had only reached the passage when Torben had turned round on the stairs and asked where he was going. 'To the bathroom,' said Chris. 'Rasmus is asleep.'

Torben had said that he was bloody unlikely to wake up for such a little thing, but Chris had gone the direct way to the bathroom and back again, without passing through Rasmus' room, just to show that he was not going to be pushed around.

But there was no hope of using the telephone. He would just have liked to ring home to say that he was all right. Perhaps he could talk Mrs Møller into letting him do it in the morning, if he promised not to say where he was?

At least these people didn't know how much he knew . . .

Chris 'put his blinkers on', as his mother called it and concentrated on the book he had borrowed from Rasmus.

54

By half-past twelve he was sleepy enough to drop off. Down below they were still arguing. He had seen their cars in the front drive from the bathroom.

Rasmus had left for school long before when Chris woke up next morning. His door was not locked, but Torben was in his place on the stairs. Chris pretended not to have seen him and went out to the bathroom. It was at least some satisfaction to know that Torben was fed up: in a way he was just as much a prisoner as Chris himself!

Mrs Møller came up with breakfast a quarter of an hour later. Chris said 'good morning' and 'thank you' politely. He had decided not to ask about anything. You got so hopping mad if people wouldn't answer. But Mrs Møller offered the information that he would have to stay with them that day as well. She had bags under her eyes and only just managed a smile.

'You could let that Torben run errands,' said Chris. 'There's no need for you to wait on me yourself.'

'But you would rather see me, wouldn't you? Since you have to see someone, I mean.'

Chris nodded.

Mrs Møller said that that was settled, then, and asked if he liked small children, because if he would like to play with Tina a bit while she was tidying the house and washing up, it would be a help.

'I certainly will. But Mrs Møller, wouldn't you let me ring my home? Just to say I'm all right, of course.'

Mrs Møller thought for a while, pushing the hair back from her forehead. It fell back again. 'I daren't, Christopher,' she said quietly. 'You see, if the police have tapped your parents' telephone—'

Chris said rather quickly that it was quite all right, he had not thought of that.

'You're a good boy, Christopher, and I'm sick of all this. My husband is too, now.'

She went, without waiting for an answer. There was no answer he could give, anyway, except that Mr Møller should have thought about it beforehand, since he couldn't even rely on the people he was doing his kidnapping with.

Rasmus turned out to have a delightful little sister. She didn't know much, of course, but she was certainly not stupid; and she was happy and playful all the time, and enjoyed everything, whether you read aloud to her or played with the farmyard or drew.

When it was twelve o'clock and he wanted to hear the radio news, he got her started on drawing a lion and he drew one at the same time. He was certain that *he* had never paid attention to the radio news when he was five years old – and he had to hear it.

All they said was that the kidnappers had not been in touch, and that the police would be brought in at six o'clock that evening unless Chris had arrived home by then, or unless they had at least heard from him.

He switched off again and made haste to admire Tina's lion. She noticed at once when he failed to pay attention, but that was probably a good thing, because he could end up by going completely nuts, just sitting and thinking. It would be great to be home, but he was not looking forward in the least to seeing Rasmus' father and mother arrested.

'Rasmus will be back early from school today,' said Mrs Møller, when she brought up his lunch. Chris did not think he could say that he didn't really care, but he didn't. He preferred little Tina. Rasmus might be all right when it came to the point, but he wasn't the kind of boy you would choose as a friend. He was too bad-tempered and too selfish, it was always a question of what *he* wanted

56

to do, and *his* feelings which had to be considered. Oh well, perhaps he wasn't always as bad as this. One had to remember that he was angry on his father's behalf just now and at the same time he was forced to put up with a boy whom he was sure he could not stand. Only it was so illogical to make up your mind about people beforehand.

A couple of hours later, Chris did it himself.

Rasmus was in high good humour when he came home, and they had just decided to 'tackle the maths', as he put it, when a car hooted outside. Chris was listening to Rasmus with half an ear. He had got a star for the homework they had done together yesterday. Someone was coming in downstairs. He could hear Mrs Møller, and another woman's voice, as well as Torben.

'You're not even listening!' Rasmus gazed at him in annoyance. Chris apologized and said that in fact he was quite interested in what was going on. At that moment Mrs Møller called 'Christopher!' from downstairs.

Chris took a quick stride towards the door, then thought better of it and walked out normally. The police could not have found him yet, because they were only to start searching last night. And it was no one else's business to know how much he was looking forward to being found and getting all this over.

'Christopher . . . you've got to . . . someone's come for you.' Mrs Møller smiled at him, but her eyes looked rather anxious. 'I . . . well, this is Yutta, and Pierre . . .' Her voice was suddenly irritable: 'For goodness sake, say hallo to Christopher, Yutta!'

The wretched woman was standing there, talking French! The man she spoke to, whose name was Pierre, nodded hastily to Chris and smiled, before turning back to listen. The woman called Yutta just looked at him as if he were an object and said hallo indifferently.

'It's been decided that you are to spend the night

somewhere else, Christopher,' said Mrs Møller. 'It's . . . well, it's more practical, you see. I think it's only for one night.'

Yutta said they must leave immediately, because she had a meeting that evening. Chris looked from one to the other. He had not said anything yet, because there was nothing to say. Rasmus stood looking foolish on the next lowest step and at that very moment, when no one was speaking, Tina came out of the room with a toy rabbit under her arm. She stopped and gazed at them all in surprise.

'Go and find our lions, Tina. Rasmus would love to see them,' said Chris quickly. The little sister nodded eagerly and rushed up the stairs, and Mrs Møller turned to Yutta. 'Well, you must be able to spare ten minutes,' she said, in the kind of voice one uses when one is really angry but doesn't want to show it. 'The boy is not simply to be hauled away without so much as a toothbrush, is he? Come on, Christopher, we'll go and see if Rasmus has a clean shirt for you too, and a pair of socks which might do.'

The woman shrugged her shoulders and began talking away in French again, while Chris went upstairs with Mrs Møller and Rasmus followed slowly.

'Let me see . . . you're a little thinner than Ras, it had better be a T-shirt.' Mrs Møller was standing with her back to him, rummaging in a drawer. 'This green one with the roll neck – yes, and a pair of socks, all right?'

Chris bit his lip – should he? 'Mrs Møller . . . I'd rather stay where I am, if you don't mind.'

Mrs Møller turned and said quickly that naturally *she* had nothing against it, 'but . . . my husband isn't home yet, so we can't talk about it together, and we have to do as we're told, don't we?' She tried to smile, but it was not a great success and Chris did not smile back. '*You* have

58

to,' he said. 'I'm only forced to, because you have taken me away from my parents. At home I'm not used to having to obey without the right to know why.'

Her eyes grew quite big and shiny and Chris could feel an enormous yawn on the way. Cripes – he was making a woman cry! 'I'll get my toothbrush,' he said hastily.

He might just as well go to the lavatory too, in order to have a moment when he could think in peace and quiet. There were four grown-ups, two men and two women. Mrs Møller certainly wouldn't do anything now, but Yutta looked capable of absolutely anything. Cripes, she was really repellent, with that bossy voice and eyes like pebbles in winter! He considered whether he should take a chance, but there wasn't one, not against four, not at a moment when they must be *expecting* him to try.

There were three of Tina's coloured marbles in the soap-dish on the hand basin. The lavatory paper was the old-fashioned, yellowish kind. Chris quickly wrote down the Møllers' name and address and added 'Yours, Christopher Egstrup'. Then he took five sheets from the roll and put it all in his trouser pocket.

If an opportunity did arise, at least he would be ready.

Rasmus was ready too, standing there with his case and two sleeping-bags, looking tense and excited, while Mrs Møller and that hideous female argued. 'Well, I don't care!' said Mrs Møller heatedly. 'Since they've got their sleeping bags, it doesn't matter to you whether you take one or two, and I say Rasmus is going! We agree about the cause, but obviously not about the method. I don't like seeing the boy being pushed around, like a piece of furniture that has to be moved, without even having a companion to talk to!'

Yutta shrugged her shoulders and was about to answer, when Chris saw Torben catch her eye and nod slightly

59

behind Mrs Møller's back. 'Oh well, for heaven's sake, let him come, then.'

That wasn't what she had intended to say, Chris was certain. What sort of foxy tricks were they up to now?

There was no time to think about it, because the Frenchman, who had not understood a word they were saying, looked impatient and said something, and Torben handed Mrs Møller a little suitcase: 'Would you take that out to the car? And how about you, Chris, will you walk out by yourself, or shall we put a hand over your mouth and carry you?'

'I can walk by myself, thanks,' said Chris sharply.

They contented themselves with walking close on either side of him, but that was enough to make Chris want to kick himself free, from pure rage. He didn't do it. They would have caught him before he had gone thirty metres, and they would have been warned then. It was better for them to think he was a zombie, as Rasmus had called him.

It was a tradesman's van, a grey Renault. Chris noted the number in a flash, and sighed inwardly. Not a chance of edging a window open and throwing something out.

They climbed into the back, following the Frenchman, who positioned himself between them and the driving seat, and Torben slammed the door behind them and locked it. 'There are some bits of carpet you can sit on,' he said, when he had taken his place beside the woman at the wheel.

'You've got your sleeping-bags, too,' Mrs Møller reminded them through the window. 'Be sensible now, boys. And – well, goodbye then, Christopher.'

Christopher said goodbye. You didn't get anywhere by being rude. On the contrary, it was almost the only thing you could protect yourself with – their not being able to make you lose your head and behave badly, or get so worried that they could see it.

The Frenchman began to drop off, his back propped against the front seat. Rasmus talked at first, but Chris answered as little as possible and bit by bit the other boy left off.

Perhaps it wasn't particularly fair – there was nothing Rasmus could do about it – but on the other hand Chris thought it was asking too much for him to make an effort and be sociable as well. In any case, he had enough to do, sneaking a few looks at his compass and watch. They drove and drove. For a time they were driving south-west, and then west for an hour and a half. It would soon be dark now.

'It's too dark to read now.' Torben yawned and put down his book: 'I don't feel like it now, anyway. Is Pierre asleep, Rasmus? What would you all say to a sausage?'

Rasmus said it 'sure as shit' sounded good, but the ugly female broke in irritably: 'Surely that isn't necessary, Torben, why complicate matters? It would be no fun for any of us if we have to knock the boy on the floor to stop him shouting for help.'

'Chris?' Torben grinned. 'He won't damn well shout. He may be a zombie, but he's not daft, and with a locked door on one side and Pierre on the other he's not going to make any trouble, are you, Chris? You intend to stay sitting on your flat rump and waiting for your little Gestapo friends, the police, to come and take you home to Mothah!'

'Oh shut up, Torben,' said Rasmus crossly. Chris closed his eyes and said nothing.

'Okay! But we'll damn well have some sausages, my friends! Now if you park here in the dark, when I tell you, I know where there is a hot-dog stand quite near by. You wait here nicely until I come back with the stuff!'

The ugly female sighed, but did as he said. Actually she wasn't ugly, Chris thought, behind closed eyelids. She was quite smart, and her face could have been pretty if only she had not looked so spiteful. Torben seemed quite harmless by comparison.

Suddenly Rasmus spoke out of the darkness: 'Where are we going actually, Yutta?'

'Think what you're saying, Rasmus! One would never believe you had played Cops and Robbers.' Even when she was presumably trying to sound pleasant, there was something disagreeably sneering in her voice.

'Chris isn't the enemy, God damn it! He's only a hostage, isn't he?'

Chris would very much have liked to hear her answer to that, but just then Torben came back. They had two hot dogs each and there was a tin of orange juice for Rasmus and him, and beer for the grown-ups. The adults talked French together while they ate.

'Are you still cross?' asked Rasmus rather warily, his mouth full of sausage.

'Yes.'

'Well, but it's shitting funny!'

'Yes, I hope you don't die laughing,' Chris snapped irritably.

Rasmus moved a little in the darkness, a little further away. He did not answer, and Chris regretted having snapped. After all, Rasmus could not do anything about it and earlier, when Torben had been nasty, he had shut him up. In fact he meant to defend me, Chris thought. And it was the same when he told that hideous commandant-type that I was not an enemy, only a hostage.

But can't he understand that I'm not too keen about being 'only a hostage'? They go on so much about Rights. Why can none of them see that no one has the right to turn other people into 'only a hostage'? No one can have an opinion which is so right that it entitles them to take hostages just to force others to think as they do.

And what, he wondered, was Rasmus?

Chris thought about Torben, who had made a sign to the spiky female behind Mrs Møller's back. She had not wanted to take Rasmus, but he had made her do it. Mrs Møller had said that morning that her husband was also sick of it now. The others had deceived him and written a different letter to NATO, one that he would not have agreed to. Why had Pierre and the woman been in such a hurry to get away? Was it because they did not want to risk Mr Møller's returning before they had gone? Perhaps Mr Møller really had no idea that they had come – was it possible that Rasmus was also a hostage now, without knowing it?

Cripes, how mad he would be, if so! But it was Mrs Møller herself who – yes, but that was only because she thought it was heartless of the others to move him about like this, and it would be nicer if he had someone to talk to. Perhaps, without knowing it, she had played right into their hands, and Torben had been quick enough to see it . . .

They had been driving southwards as soon as they started off again after the hot-dog break. Chris hung on tightly when the van took a sharp turn. Eastwards now. He frowned. Should he say something to Rasmus? No, that had better wait until they were alone. But he must take care not to let his imagination run away with him. Torben was a real activist, but he was a perfectly straightforward Dane, not some extraordinary monster.

He had bought sausages for all of them, including Chris. It *might* even be possible that he had only chipped in about Rasmus because he thought Mrs Møller had a little bit of right on her side.

'We seem to be driving round and round an awful lot,'

63

said Rasmus suddenly, his voice loud in the darkness. The female answered without turning her head: 'We are. We must be there by six, but it has to be dark before we arrive.'

Rasmus gave vent to a rather embarrassed 'Mmm, well . . .' but Chris almost gasped aloud. So Rasmus *had* been kidnapped as well! Otherwise why on earth would they have been in such a sweat to leave the Møllers' house, just to drive round and round so that it would be dark before they arrived – unless because they had not discussed his removal with Mr Møller at all and were certain that he would not agree?

This was so logical that even Rasmus must see it! Chris almost held his breath in terror that he was going to say something. As long as *they* believed that Rasmus believed that he had gone of his own free will, just to keep Chris company, the chances of getting away would be better. Because they had to get out of this, and the sooner the better. The Møllers were one thing, but she, the female, was capable of absolutely anything, and it was obviously she who gave all the orders.

Chris tried to think out what he really meant by 'absolutely anything', but without success. There were just a whole lot of unconnected thoughts, all linked with something disagreeable, something which made him yawn.

'We're nearly there now,' said the female. 'I'm going to blindfold you – Torben and Pierre will help you inside so that you don't fall.'

Rasmus got annoyed at once, saying that he 'was damn well not going to have a blindfold on'.

'Oh, yes, you will. Christian isn't allowed to see where we are, is he? So you might just as well be pals together.'

She was almost worse now, when she was pretending

64

to be jolly, thought Chris. Aloud he said: 'My name is Christopher.'

'Oh well, Christopher then.'

Rasmus wasn't even suspicious! Chris attempted to see his face in the darkness. You could hear from his voice that he thought it was all a joke when Pierre covered his eyes.

Chris didn't find it the least bit amusing. Pierre made some friendly noises and you could just make out that he was smiling. But he was a little too practised in tying bandages over people's eyes for Chris's taste.

5

If only all this had been a dream, it could almost have been exciting. Chris turned over a little on the odd piece of furniture, which resembled some kind of old-fashioned sofa that had never been finished off. Cripes, how it creaked!

It *did* feel like something which could not be happening in reality, something you saw in pictures or read about in historical novels about conspirators and so on. How could there be such a huge attic as a single room? He had counted the steps when Torben helped them up and they must be at least on the third floor of a house. It was horrible having a bandage over your eyes. Rasmus could certainly not have enjoyed it either, even if he had played the clown.

Chris had felt no desire to do that. He had been so

angry that he could not even yawn his way out of it. He had simply shuddered with cold, so much that he was aware of gooseflesh all over his body.

'What the hell, are you scared? There's no damn reason to be scared, you little stinker,' Torben had said.

Chris had replied that he was not scared, he was cold, and Torben had said 'Well, yes, the car had been pretty damn cold'. In his blustering way he was not too bad, or at least, compared with that female, he seemed to be some kind of human. She was not. She spoke better than he did with no off-beat words, but one couldn't imagine her having normal, ordinary thoughts inside her head, about everyday things. She spoke as if it had all been removed by surgery and replaced by a machine which simply spat out political jargon all the time.

They were exactly like conspirators in an old-fashioned book, sitting down there – or rather lying – some of them, in any case. *Mumble-mumble-mumble* went the talk, and the faces looked strange in the light of the candle flames. What was the point of sitting or lying in a circle round the tiny little fire of candles, when there were plenty of standard lamps around them? Was this room really twenty metres long? Perhaps only fifteen. But quite low, and the windows quite small. There were a lot of them, but curtains hung over them all. Oh well, now it was evening there wouldn't have been much to see in any case.

They had had sausages for supper. Rasmus had been blissful, and the sausages *were* good, it wasn't that. But once a day was enough – and the way some of them ate! The one called Viggo, for instance, and the one called Mick. But the one whose name was Henning had been the worst, because you could see that he had certainly learned to eat properly once. He was quite middle-aged, almost the same age as Father, and the one called Carl was even older. Viggo and Mick were young; not very young, but about the same as Jørgen and his friends. The one called Henrik was the nicest looking, but he seemed strangely confused, as if he could never make up his mind about anything. But he had been pleasant and chatty.

Now, I must take care not to be as old-fashioned and capitalistic as they think I am, thought Chris. How could you be capitalistic, by the way, when you were thirteen years old and had nothing but pocket money? But I mustn't judge people by whether they are pleasant to eat with. And they have a right to hold what opinions they like . . . even if I think they are rubbish.

But then he was back where he started. You had the right to an opinion, and also to form new Parties and get into Parliament, so that you could help to decide on the law. But you could not have any rights over other people. You had no right to forbid others to disagree with you, and you had no right to steal people, whether they were children or grown-ups.

No, stop! Now he was getting around to the thing he absolutely definitely ought not to think about. Better start thinking with his eyes, as Mother called it.

Chris removed his gaze from the chattering group further down the room and began to describe it to himself: I don't know how long the room is, but it is not very wide, probably not more than five metres. All those small windows on one long wall – ten of them. Beams in the low ceiling. Furniture of different kinds along all the walls, mostly cabinets of different sizes against the long wall. A lot of chairs, not matching, but some of them at least must have been very handsome once. Four tables, one very large, the others smaller. Two beds here at this end, end to end under the window, with mattresses on them, and some others standing on end against the opposite wall. Beside the battered sofa he was lying on

67

was a bureau which must have been very pretty once, before the top began to break up. Oh yes, what all the things had in common was that they were broken, or else old-fashioned in a funny way, so that you could not imagine having them in a proper room. That lamp on the bureau, for instance, with a bulging shade of gathered light-blue silky stuff and long, shaggy fringes round the edge. It was like an enormous lumber room – and of course, that was just what it was!

Chris's eyes rested on something standing under the window a little way off, near where the others were sitting. A rocking-horse. A very large rocking-horse, true to life and painted white. He had seen one like that only once before . . .

Chris yawned and got to his feet. He fiddled with the fringes on the light-blue lampshade for a moment, took a few more steps and stopped to look at a painting leaning against the wall. It was of a lady in the kind of clothes which had been modern several hundred years ago, with a silly hair-style, a rose in her hair and a little dog in her arms. There was a great gash in the top right-hand corner of the painting.

Torben had watched when he got up, then looked away again.

Chris ambled on, strolled over to the opposite wall where there was a peculiar wooden stand – then he had reached the rocking-horse. The right-hand glass eye was missing.

Nice old Baron Corfeldt of 'Marieholm' was a kidnapper and activist . . . !

Rasmus called to him to join the others and Torben said the same, but Chris shook his head, with a little lop-sided smile to show that he was not really cross, and went back to the half-sofa.

That fine old gentleman, whom he had visited last

summer with his mother and father, and who had been so kind and courteous, even to boys, who knew all kinds of things about everything possible and talked just as intelligently about music and politics as about old Chinese porcelain and – but was the whole world upside down? When they drove away Mother had said that it was refreshing to find that there were still people of Baron Corfeldt's type 'even if he is too stuck in his ideas of a bygone age'.

It was because – yes, why was it? Ah yes, he lived in France, or somewhere, in the winter, not to be capitalistic but, on the contrary, because he had not enough money to buy fuel for the big manor house. 'The house can get by at 12–14 degrees without the contents being damaged, but my old lungs can't,' he had said. And he thought it was important that not all the stately homes in Denmark should be turned into offices or museums, and that was why he didn't want to sell Marieholm. But when Mother said he was too old-fashioned, it was because he could not bear to take money to let part of his house in France, although he could scarcely keep that up any more either, owing to taxes. He used to lend the house to other old people who were poor.

'And there surely can't be any point in that old man having to eat porridge all week, just because he is too stubborn to recognize that times have changed since he was young!'

Mother could not bear porridge.

Cripes, if she had only known! But at least *he* now knew where he was. Up in the attics at Marieholm Hall. That would fit in very well with the direction in which they had driven and the time they had taken.

'Hey, Christopher! Don't you want to see the news?' That was Torben.

Chris went over to the others and Rasmus made a place for him on the mattress between himself and Torben.

Not very much was said, only that 'all available police' had been put on to the search for 'the Prime Minister's thirteen-year-old son Christopher Egstrup' since eight o'clock, and that there were still no clues to follow. Anyone who had seen him after he had left the Chess Club was to ring the police.

But there had been no one, not even the hot-dog seller.

They had not heard from the kidnappers. There was a hazy picture of Father just getting into the car, while the driver held the door. A journalist was asking him if he had anything to say about the kidnapping and Father turned and said 'No comment'. He was not smiling, but he looked calm, just as he always did, fortunately.

And then there was a picture of himself! It filled the screen. It was his passport picture, which had been taken last week for the skiing trip with the school after Christmas. Cripes, what *did* he look like! It was all glasses, apart from the grin. Jørgen had been standing behind the camera, playing the clown. That one was a little better; Mother had taken that on the verandah one day while he was playing chess with Father. The speaker said he was 158 cm tall, and broad-shouldered, but otherwise of average build and that he had dark brown hair, blue eyes and a clear skin.

Cripes, how idiotic, that bit about the skin. But perhaps they had to do it so that people didn't start looking for a boy with spots. All the same, it was going to be jolly awkward on his first day back at school after this business was over.

There was a strange silence for quite a long moment when the one called Carl switched off the set, as if they were all suddenly wondering what to say.

'Well, well, it's nice to know that you haven't got spots,' said the female finally. 'I must say, I hadn't noticed that.'

Chris swallowed back a yawn. 'No,' he said coolly. 'But you're in too much of a hurry to notice very much, aren't you? You have no time to remember the names of the children you kidnap, and when Rasmus' little sister came running up to show you her rabbit you were in too much of a hurry even to give her a smile and say it was lovely.'

Once again there was a short, heavy silence. Then Henning suddenly pretended to have been seized with despair, tore his hair and moaned: 'Oh God! Are we supposed to be child-lovers, too! I, who hate children! My friends, there must be limits to what the revolution asks of its sons.'

What a stupid ass he was! And yet there was something almost familiar about his face, as if one had seen him before, perhaps in pictures? If only these people could at least say their names; the only thing they tossed to one was a first name—

Chris began to laugh at himself; he was the one who was being illogical now. One could hardly expect them to give their names and addresses, so that he had only to learn them by heart and tell the police later!

Now they were all talking again. The female was talking French to Pierre; she must have been translating what had been said in the News, and Carl's deep voice was droning on at the same time – how he talked, that man!

Suddenly Chris met Torben's eyes.

Once in a while you could see what someone else was thinking. For a split second you could see through their eyes into their thoughts as certainly as if they had been speaking aloud.

Torben was thinking with surprise: 'He is a boy. His name is Christopher and at home they call him Chris. He has glasses and brown hair and he is thirteen years old, as

I was once. He plays games after school and he is good at chess. He is not an object, he is a real live boy.'

Chris went on looking into his eyes and saw that Torben did not like the thoughts he was having.

I could at least have smiled at him, it would have soothed him a bit, thought Chris later. But why should I soothe him? If all this mess could make him wake up and at least listen to opinions other than his own, then my being a laughing-stock to the whole country won't be entirely wasted!

Not long afterwards Torben got up and went out of the door and Henrik, the nicest looking of the three young men, came over and sat down in his place. 'Shall we share an orange?' he said, taking one out of his pocket. It was Chris who peeled it. At the very last moment he remembered to say that he had forgotten his penknife and would have to borrow one. Not that he could imagine at this moment what use a penknife would be to him in the attics of Marieholm, with a single heavy door leading to freedom and a whole mob of adults to guard it, but just in case – no one was going to know that he had a first-class knife in his pocket.

Torben came back with a bundle of newspapers. 'Here, you! There weren't any at the Møllers' this morning – and there is a bulb in that pale blue atrocity over there!'

Chris managed to say thank you and take the papers before Yutta asked what the boy wanted with newspapers. 'He's already seen his picture once today!'

'Hold your tongue, Yutta!' said Torben shortly. 'Mogens and Inger were right about that, at least. We're damned well not making war on children, and Christopher hasn't done a shitting thing to us. On the contrary, the poor wretch goes round being polite, although it almost chokes him! No one can damned well expect him to be

72

whooping with enthusiasm, and it doesn't matter if he does see what's going on.'

'Quite! Or rather, Yutta . . .' – this was Carl – '. . . the boy's sojourn in our group may be precisely the thing to create a dialogue and become a relevant correction of Philistine denigrations . . .'

Whatever he meant by that!

Chris got to his feet. 'I'll move now, so that you can discuss me and my behaviour in peace,' he said.

At last it was night again! Chris turned cautiously in the bed, which creaked if one didn't take care. He could not sleep: when you were allowed to sleep on in the morning until you woke up by yourself, you were even wider awake at night. It didn't matter, anyway. There would certainly be people here at night as well, both Rasmus and some of the others were sleeping here. But as long as they lay still, kept quiet and slept, you could at least pretend that you were alone.

It's an extraordinary feeling that everything you are and think is quite wrong, thought Chris. Rasmus is having a wonderful time; though he was put out for a moment in the afternoon, when he wanted to go for a walk and was not allowed to. Well, of course they didn't say that, and as soon as they reminded him that he was here to be with me and not to 'go gadding about' he agreed and made no more fuss. Otherwise he's having a wonderful time, talking and arguing and being mixed up in it all. And it's not just because I haven't yet told him that he has really been kidnapped as well – he simply likes being in a crowd all the time.

I can't stand it. I always thought that business about communes sounded pretty awful, but it's worse than that. When you're camping with the school, or on a trip or something, it's great fun – for a few days or a week or

73

even a fortnight, but after all, you *choose* to go, knowing that you are going to be living a communal life for a short time only. And you are busy with things to see or do.

Here there's no end to it; it's quite difficult to remember what day it is! There's always *someone* and one of them is always talking or fooling about, or eating, or sleeping. Things you need are suddenly somewhere else, not where you put them yourself. If you wash your own plate, it's messy again when you want to use it. There's never anyone who works the other way round – well, Henrik, sometimes. Sometimes he washes a whole stack, but he doesn't get them particularly clean. And all that bickering all the time about unimportant things, because no one can make up their minds to a practical arrangement about anything, or keep to it if they have one. But certainly the worst thing of all is simply that there is *always* someone.

Rasmus could stand it. The grown-ups didn't seem to have anything against it either, as far as he could see. Chris frowned. Henrik said it was a blessing. He said that 'it was only when you lived as part of other people that you became a real human being'.

If that were true, I would never be one, thought Chris despondently. But I don't believe it. It may be true for him, but it can't be true for everyone; you must have the right to be different!

And here, you haven't. They were quite different in themselves but on that they were like a brick wall: you could only have an opinion if it was the same opinion as theirs.

Torben had left in the evening. It was very odd that in only two days one had got round to thinking of him as some kind of safeguard. Rasmus was only a boy, after all, and the others – the others felt strangely unreal, as if they had never been outside in wind and weather, out in the world like normal people. They just sat there on the floor talking, talking, about the revolution and the Third World and 'the lackeys of Imperialism' and 'the Establishment' and about how they would destroy everything. Sometimes one would go and get some food or go to the lavatory and when it began to get dark they lighted all the candles, but they talked all the time about the same thing.

Luckily Torben had taken the female with him. I'm afraid of her, thought Chris. It sounds quite crazy, because she's only a grown-up girl.

They had not watched television that evening. The night before, the only news was that the hunt for the kidnappers was continuing and that 'the police were following up several clues'. Then of course the female had said that it was typical of 'the tools of a rotten government, to keep the population in the dark!' And the next evening, Carl was so busy talking that no one had noticed the time.

He had pretended that he really wanted to talk to Chris, but it wasn't true. To begin with Chris had believed him, because Carl had actually asked him what he thought. Chris had answered, and he had taken some trouble over it. Father always said that a child could not expect an adult to be interested in what he thought if he could not finish his sentences, instead of letting them trickle away half-way through with 'er . . . I mean, you know?'

Of course he had opposed Carl, but he had done it logically and in complete sentences. The only thing was that Carl was not really the slightest bit interested in other people's opinions. When he said he wanted to talk to you, what he really meant was that he wanted to talk *at* you. He sat staring fiercely into one's eyes as if he were terribly interested, but it was only in order to be ready to snatch at some particular word in what one was saying and interrupt, so that he could go on with what he was determined to say.

So one didn't bother any more.

Viggo and Mick were at least not hypocritical, they just talked on and on, taking it for granted that other people's opinions were wrong and therefore unimportant. Viggo was apparently studying to be a social worker and Mick was at film school because he wanted to be a film director. It must be difficult, because he would have nothing to do with those teachers at the school who were what he called 'part of the Establishment' and one of them taught camera technique. And he would never have actual actors in his film, he said.

How could you get strangers to pay money to see your films, when you would neither learn how to make them nor have anyone who could really act?

It was the same with Viggo, but in a different way. As a social worker he should be helping people to find out about the law so that they could use it properly. But Viggo 'had no respect for the so-called laws of a capitalist society', he said.

So the law would have to be changed first, before he could do anything. Chris turned over in bed again, wishing he could go to sleep quickly, because apart from Henning's wife or whatever she was, there would soon be no one left to think about but Henning himself.

Her name was Ellen. There wasn't really very much about her that you *could* think of. She was moody: one moment she was giggling and pert and noisy and half an hour later she was being sour and spiteful to them all. But there was something unreal about both sides, as if she were simply acting a mood. She went about in a mini-length dress with jingly things and little mirrors on it. It would have looked better if she had worn a skirt or trousers underneath it, because she had thick, ugly legs.

It was half-past two in the morning now. Would Father and Mother and Jørgen be sleeping? Probably not very well, at all events; they could not have imagined that anyone could go on being kidnapped for days, here in Denmark.

He hadn't thought so himself, either.

But what could he do? There was so little he *could* do – he could only wait. Hold on secretly to the small advantages he had, so that they might count at the right moment – and wait. Not lose patience, not let himself be provoked so that they found out that he was not quite such a zombie as they thought. And above all, not get into a panic. Try to forget that the whole thing was not a very poor, thoughtless kind of joke; not even some kind of illogical, unreal nonsense which could not really be happening. Illogical, confused, pointless, yes. But it *could* be happening. It was on Thursday night that he had been on his way home from the Chess Club in the wind and darkness, when the book-seller was decorating the window on the corner. Tomorrow would be Tuesday. Sometimes one suddenly felt that the book-seller on the corner of the avenue was no longer there, that the Chess Club was merely something one had dreamed, and that Father and Mother and Jørgen and the world outside which he had always known had simply ceased to exist.

Or that *I* don't exist any more, thought Chris. The boy who had been on his way home after playing chess, looking forward to tea and sandwiches and talk under the big, warm, yellow lamp – that he simply was not. That on the way, by the Tystrups' chestnut tree, he had been turned into some object which you stored in the Marie-holm attics, beside the one-eyed rocking-horse.

A bunch of grown-up strangers couldn't accept the law, so they tried to smash it instead, by taking a live boy

77

and turning him into a thing to be shut away behind a locked attic door.

There is one of them who hates me. It was like a little hard black bullet somewhere in his stomach when he thought about it, but it was true. The one called Henning hates me. I don't know why – I can't even think of a reason, because how can a man hate a stranger, a boy of thirteen? But he does. The others – apart from Henrik – simply hate everything. They go on talking all the time about the good there is to be done and about how the whole world is going to be just and fine, when they have their way, but when they talk about *how* they will do it they plan nothing but hatred and force and destruction.

But their hatred is general. They don't hate me, I've just become an object. Henning hates *me*. I can see it in his eyes – he thinks evil when he looks at me. His smile is never real, it's a movement he makes with his mouth, not something which comes because he's amused or wants to make his face friendly towards somebody. But when it's me he's smiling at, he actually makes sure that I shall see it's only a grimace.

Chris jumped as Rasmus turned over noisily in the bed in front of him. This kind of thing got on your nerves in the end! If only there had been someone to talk to – but it was no use talking to Rasmus, or not for the time being, at least. He was having a good time, and if Chris could convince him that he was just as much kidnapped as himself, he would lose his temper and give the whole show away. Not that there was much to give away, just a few little advantages the others didn't know about. But they must not be wasted at a moment when nothing could possibly be done.

There was so much you could do in a thriller, Chris thought irritably. The author took care to arrange a way out: here there was none. A big, heavy door with keys and two bolts. And outside it, when you were taken to the lavatory, there was another big, heavy, locked door. If only he could have smuggled out a message; but underneath the windows there was nothing but the home park of Marieholm, and no one came there. He had watched for hours.

There was nothing to do but wait, and stick to the chess board. Torben had brought it before he left. Henning's face had looked very strange for a moment: it was in fact a very, very precious, rare set. Baron Corfeldt had shown it to Chris himself last summer, but Chris didn't care. Much good might it do him, the traitor! The others at least admitted that they were the country's enemies, but the Baron was a regular spy, making use of the fact that other people believed he was a dear old man, and an ordinary person.

Not that Chris intended to be careless with the chess pieces, of course. It would be illogical to destroy something beautiful and rare, simply because it belonged to someone one despised.

White was made of crystal and black was really green, because it was carved out of jade. Was the Baron getting money for this? He should have sold the chess set instead, and gone on being a nice old gentleman.

He had to sleep; if I go on thinking about the beautiful chessmen, perhaps I won't have such horrible dreams as yesterday, thought Chris. Henning's hair, which was long, and straggled down his neck. The nails, bitten short, on Henning's fingers, which were always grabbing and grasping at the air as he spoke. Henning's teeth, when he did his smile-grimace. Henning's strangely high, flat voice, saying: 'I've heard that small boys taste very good with mayonnaise.'

It was just a silly dream.

6

When Chris woke up it was quite light. It must be almost morning. A little thin sunshine was coming through the front window; Christmas was not far off. If something didn't happen soon he would not be home by the time they were making the Advent wreath. It was such a cheerful time: you pricked yourself like mad on the pine needles and there was always a thin patch left somewhere, or the wreath was crooked, and he and Jørgen baked a gingerbread man each, for fun, as they had done when they were little, and probably Mother would have forgotten how many candles they needed for the holders and they would have to go into town for more. And then at last there was darkness and tea and gingerbread men and the proper Christmas biscuits – the first batch, that is – came to the table and Father lighted the first candle.

Chris yawned. Next Sunday it would be Jørgen's turn, and the one after that, his own. And on the last Sunday Mother lighted the candles, because then it was almost Christmas and after all she was the one who saw to it that everything was properly Christmassy.

If only he could just become himself again, instead of an object put away in an attic.

Chris drew the curtain back from his window and discovered that Rasmus was sitting up on his bed, fully dressed, peering out of his own, his arms round his knees and his chin resting on them.

'Hallo!' he said, surprised. ' 'Morning! What's the time?'

'Half-past ten,' Rasmus grunted sulkily.

'Good Lord! Have you had anything for breakfast?' One never knew – sometimes something would be cooked on the two electric hotplates they had in here and sometimes Ellen came up with something in a basket. There was enough food, that wasn't the point, though it was mostly sandwiches, but they had had fried eggs, too, and warmed-up hot-dogs. None of the grown-ups seemed to be really hungry, they all seemed quite content to get by with a beer.

'I took an orange juice. There's a packet of crispbread, too.'

It was difficult to believe that things could have reached the point where one couldn't bear to look at a tin of orange juice, and yet they should be glad that Torben had thought of bringing up a whole lot of tins, otherwise they would have had to drink beer.

'Oh well,' said Chris mildly, beginning to pull on his socks. 'But it would have been nice to have a whole pot of tea and some of your mother's good homemade bread, wouldn't it?'

'Shut up, you shit!' Rasmus' voice was muffled. Chris reached for his glasses, turned his head and regarded Rasmus attentively.

Then he looked down the room to where the mattresses lay. Candles had been lighted and they had not even drawn back the curtains.

'What is it?' he said, lowering his voice. 'What are they doing, Rasmus?'

Rasmus said he didn't damn well know, and looked out of the window.

Chris took another look. 'They're scarcely talking at

81

all,' he said. 'You idiot! Can't you even guess? I'm sure *I* can!'

'They – well, one or two of them have had a shot – the others are just smoking.' Rasmus tried to sound careless, but was not entirely successful.

'Cripes, what a filthy mess!' He meant it. But perhaps he should have said it a little more . . . a little less . . . oh well, luckily Rasmus did not seem to have noticed.

'It's, well, it's to do with expanding consciousness, you know,' he explained.

'Stuff that!' said Chris shortly. 'You don't know a thing about it – I hope. You're just repeating what you've heard the grown-ups saying. That's what you always accuse me of doing! But I can't see any expansion of consciousness in that flock of owls over there! They haven't even realized that it's light and that the sun is shining a little, not to speak of forgetting that children you snatch and lock in can't live on orange juice and crispbread!'

Rasmus raised his head and looked at him. 'What the devil do you mean by that?' he asked, his eyes watchful.

Chris thought there was nothing to be done but tell him. Perhaps this was the right moment. Rasmus was obviously not nearly as offhand about the use of narcotics as he liked to pretend.

He wasn't stupid, either, and when Chris asked if he could think of any other reason why they had been picked up from his mother's so early in the afternoon that the fe— that Yutta had had to drive round and round for hours so that they would not arrive before dark, Rasmus had no answer.

'But why the hell . . .'

'Sssh! Don't make a noise, you fool! Suppose they hear us!'

Rasmus lowered his voice. 'But why should they? Can you possibly tell me that?'

82

'Yes, I certainly can,' said Chris. 'They double-crossed your father, didn't they? I could tell that quite clearly on the first evening. The letter *your* father wrote to *my* father when they conned me into being a hostage . . . that wasn't the one they sent, was it? Your father had demanded a referendum over the NATO business; I have no idea if that would have been possible, but at least there is nothing illegal about a referendum. But the letter the others sent instead was quite different. That demanded something from Father which he simply cannot do.'

'No one could damn well stop him getting up and saying anything he liked, since he's Prime Minister,' Rasmus objected scornfully.

Chris was ready to tear his hair out. 'Do you have to be as thick as a double door? Of course it's not that. He can go up there and sing rude songs or make his wife the heir to the throne or declare war against Sweden or Australia if he likes. But even before they had got him out of the Speaker's chair he would have stopped being Prime Minister, I can tell you. And the Government would have folded, or retired, or whatever it is. A Prime Minister is not a dictator; the moment he did something insane like that he would be out!'

'There's nothing insane about withdrawing from NATO,' said Rasmus, scowling.

Chris said mildly that that might well be, he himself didn't know enough about it and in any case, that was not what they were discussing. 'What *is* insane is to be Prime Minister and then to say something which is against the law from the Speaker's chair. Quite apart from the fact,' Chris added thoughtfully, 'that I think they would have to make a new law about it, and Father couldn't sign it all on his own even if he wanted to, because the Queen has to sign new laws!'

'The Queen!'

If they had not been in such a hurry, Chris would have laughed. Rasmus had quite a large mouth and when he grimaced like that it almost split his face in half.

'The Queen is pretty good, so Father says, but that's not the point, is it? I know it's more trendy to be Republican, but I think it's a very good thing to have a King or Queen, because then you can be sure they sign because they want to, and not because someone has promised them a good post or something if they do. And they can't go off and do things on their own if they suddenly feel like it, without asking anyone. Nor can my father, and that's what we're talking about.'

'Your father knows that. But that collection of savages down there haven't the slightest idea what they're talking about. It's not necessary, when you just want to throw bricks and take hostages and never consider other people. That was what they were doing when they picked me up on Saturday and seized the opportunity to get you too, just because your mother is nice and thought that things were bad enough already. Why didn't they wait until your father came home? Because he knew nothing about it and would never have agreed! Now they've got a hold over him, just as they have over my father. That's what they think.'

'But it was my mother herself who said . . .'

'Yes, and Torben was quicker off the mark than that female, he was the one who shut her mouth and made sure you came. Your mother just wanted to be nice to me, but you were locked into the van too, weren't you? And you had a blindfold over your eyes when we came up here. And you weren't allowed to go for a walk yesterday when you wanted to, were you? If your father and mother had known where you were, don't you think you would have heard from them?'

'But, but Chris—'

84

'Yes, well, of course I don't know about that last point because I don't known how much interest your father and mother take in what you're doing, but, if I had been taken away suddenly like that while he wasn't at home, my father would certainly have rung up to make sure I had enough money on me, or had remembered my spare glasses or something.'

Rasmus swung his legs to the floor. 'I'm going to ring home at once! There must be a telephone somewhere . . .'

'Rasmus! Stop!' Chris took his arm. 'Just listen, can't you? And whatever you do, don't shout!'

Rasmus stopped, but he sat down impatiently, as if on springs, so Chris would have to be brief. He leaned forward and looked into Rasmus' face. 'If I'm right, that means we're on the same side for the moment, doesn't it?'

Rasmus nodded.

'And if you yourself have been kidnapped, you won't go on thinking it's quite all right to kidnap people, will you?'

'No, you can be sure as shit about that!'

Chris sighed. Logic really wasn't Rasmus' strong point. He didn't even realize that he was admitting that there should be one law for some and another for others! But at least he was listening.

'All right. If you agree that we must try to get away if we can, the silliest thing you could do is to let the others find out that you've found *them* out. If you go over and say you want to ring up home about something, they will have to say no, and then you'll make a row and the balloon will go up, won't it? At present they think you believe you're here of your own free will. At least you can go to the lavatory alone, for instance.'

'So what?'

'Well, you can try the door to the stairs without anyone seeing – find out if it's locked, I mean.'

85

Rasmus said: 'We-ell, yes.' Chris thought his face looked rather odd for a moment, but perhaps it was the sun shining straight into his eyes.

'But don't do it right away. They mustn't suspect that we're planning something together,' warned Chris.

Rasmus said he wasn't particularly good at play-acting. He said it as if he were reluctantly revealing a great secret, and Chris grinned inwardly. As far as he could see, Rasmus never thought at all before he spoke, so the great secret did not come as a particular surprise.

'You won't have to do that. You can just be bad-tempered! If anyone asks, you can say you're getting bored. Torben at least knows we're not exactly bosom friends, doesn't he?'

Rasmus muttered something indistinct to the effect that no one had said anything like that.

'Well, but *I'm* saying it!' said Chris firmly. 'We're much, much too different. A bit of difference is a good thing, it gives you something to talk about, but we are simply basically opposed on everything. *I* think you're madly irritating and you look upon me like a bull seeing a red rag. So don't let's try to fool ourselves. But you don't have to be enemies just because you're not particularly interested in being friends. We can be good enough in ourselves, and count on the other being the same, so that we can help each other out when we're in a spot, can't we? That's what I think, anyway. But you must say if you don't want to be in on it, so that we know where we are.'

Rasmus did not answer at first, but when Chris just looked at him without saying anything more, he came out at last with a sullen: 'I'm not an idiot, am I?'

That was probably the closest Rasmus could get to admitting someone else was right, so Chris let it go at that.

Keeping their voices low, they discussed possible methods of escape for some time. At first Rasmus had various ideas about tying sheets together, signalling in morse and smuggling messages out in the dustbin. Chris had gone through all that long before.

'It won't do, Rasmus. Don't you think I've thought about all that? But there's someone here the whole time. How on earth could you tear up enough sheets to get down from the third floor without their hearing and seeing what you were up to? Quite apart from the fact that we haven't got any sheets! And as for the dustbin, in the first place they haven't got one. It's only Carl and Torben and Yutta who sometimes happen to remove the rubbish and put it outside the door to the stairs. Even if anyone collected it, the whole bag just goes straight into the District Council's furnaces without anyone looking through it first. The only thing that *might* work is morse, but we haven't got any torches, have we? And if we had – how would we signal without the others noticing?'

Rasmus sat scowling to himself, biting his thumb. 'What about nicking a lighter?' he said at last.

Chris gave him an appreciative look. 'You should go in for a bit more thinking – that's not at all a bad idea,' he said. Rasmus was just about to blow up, until he realized that he was only being teased, and subsided.

'The awful thing is, I can't really remember how to do SOS, can you?'

'Um, no . . .'

At any other time Chris would have burst out laughing, but there was nothing really funny about that moment, and in any case Rasmus was not the right person to laugh with. Things had to be quite violent before he thought they were funny.

Aloud he said: 'If you can pinch one, perhaps you

could use it from the lavatory after dark. If you stand on the seat you can reach the window. Isn't it something like two long and one short, or the other way round? Oh, hang it, you can do something like that, some irregular flashes. Even if it's wrong, it might at least attract attention. If anyone sees it, that is.'

Chris did not have much faith that anyone would see it. The park was large, and a lighter, even if they could get hold of one, could probably not even be seen as far away as the road. But there was no point in telling Rasmus that.

He hadn't said anything about where they were, either. Not that he did not trust Rasmus, but he was so apt to give things away without thinking, and Henning was cunning even if the others were too absorbed in their opinions about everything. He talked in fits and starts, sometimes like a runaway engine and sometimes not at all, but his eyes were always moving from one to another. One should not let oneself be fooled by the smile-grimace which he put on all the time, because he was obviously thinking something quite different, Chris was sure of that. The clowning was something he hid behind, and if he got suspicious of Rasmus it would be a small matter for him to winkle out every detail, without Rasmus' even realizing that he had given anything away.

'Well, I'd better be getting up. Where do you think the others wash?'

'In the bathroom, of course,' said Rasmus blankly.

Ah, then it wasn't so extraordinary that most of them smelled: seven, and sometimes ten, or even more of them, for one little hand-basin, a scrap of soap and a thin, filthy towel! He had not been able to make himself use the towel, he had dried himself on his handkerchief.

He asked Henrik first, before having a proper look at

him; you couldn't see very well when they didn't pull back the curtains. Henrik smiled at him, but with a strange vagueness, as if he could not see clearly enough to make out Chris's face, and he did not move.

'Well, so his junior excellency wishes to make water? I will escort him!'

Chris took half a step backwards and pretended not to have noticed that Henning was about to support himself on his shoulder to get up.

'You young people,' said Henning, swaying slightly as he walked ahead of him to the door, 'you young people have no stamina, you know. Henrik is a bit off colour today – understand?'

Chris stopped at the door and looked the man in the eyes. They were glowing strangely and the smile-grimace was more lopsided and senseless than ever. 'Yes, I understand!' he said.

As soon as he reached the lavatory he yawned until his jaws were almost dislocated and his chest seemed to expand half a metre. If only that – that criminal – had not been standing just outside he would have been sick; that would have helped.

He was just going to pick the soap up off the floor and turn on the tap when something occurred to him: what was it that Uncle George had said about inflammation of the liver? It was infectious, but was it contagious if you just touched something other people had touched? First you were so sick and felt so rotten that you wanted to die, and then, if you had it badly enough, you did die.

Better not take any risks: Chris put two pieces of lavatory paper on the tap before turning it, and did not touch the soap. Ugh, how it stank in here! But that was hardly surprising, since they could not even manage to pull the plug for themselves. He took hold a good way up the chain instead of using the handle and pulled it down hard.

Fortunately Henning had lost the desire to talk for the moment. His eyes had flickered when Chris looked at him. Back in the big attic, Chris said shortly: 'I suppose I can have some crispbread'. Henning just nodded, waved his hands affectedly and went back to the mattresses.

Chris took the last knob of butter and all the crispbread. What a disgusting mess there was in the cupboard! Empty tins and loose lids, greasy paper, an end of sausage, all furry with mould – ugh! But when there was nothing but crispbread and orange juice and a wrinkled apple, perhaps it was just as well that he had lost his appetite.

Ellen was lounging over there too; she could not have combed her hair since the day before. Chris stopped on his way back to Rasmus: 'There's no food left at all,' he told her. 'I'd just like you to know, in case you get hungry yourself, I mean. *I* have to put up with it.'

Rasmus was gazing out of the window again. Chris gave him the apple to peel and went to work on the crispbread himself. They sat in silence for a while, then Rasmus said:

'Look – er – if I were you, I shouldn't accept anything they offer you – I'm not sure that there might not be something mixed up in it.'

Chris was just about to get angry in earnest. Then he restrained himself: the Møllers were the kind of people who thought that hash should be made legal, and so in fact it was fair of Rasmus to have warned him, at least.

'There probably is,' Chris took a gulp of orange juice. 'I think that Henning is capable of absolutely anything! But it doesn't matter to me, because I wouldn't think of having anything to do with such muck. And if you tell me again that it's for expanding consciousness, you must be crazy. Just look at them, man!'

Rasmus was not even indignant. 'Yes, but ordinary hash isn't dangerous,' he informed Chris. 'No more than tobacco, for instance.'

'Well, I don't smoke tobacco either. I'm a zombie, as you know!' Chris smiled wrily, 'and I've had an authoritarian upbringing, as you call it. Father and Mother and my elder brother say it's healthier not to start, because if you don't start you won't miss it. Father used to smoke a cigar after dinner, but he's stopped now. Mother sometimes has a cigarette, but not every day. Jørgen smokes a pipe when he has time. So I'm dull enough to take their advice; no one will be able to tempt me, don't worry!'

'I'm not so sure you are particularly dull,' said Rasmus contrarily. 'Not like that. You're as priggish as crap and a conformist and all that, but not particularly dull.'

Chris hid his amazement as well as he could.

'You'd better watch out, too,' he retorted. 'I can't remember how you catch inflammation of the liver, but it *is* catching, and I shouldn't be surprised if they are sharing hypodermic needles – to judge from the slovenly way they do everything. I dry my hands on my handkerchief and I watch out how I hold the taps. You ought to do the same.'

Rasmus said that one should not be taken in by 'scare campaigns', and Chris said that it was better to be taken in once too often than once too little.

Both of them looked across at the mattress group, where voices were being raised. Henning had got to his feet and was tugging at Ellen to get her up. Chris heard the word 'sausages' and shuddered. Even Rasmus sighed at the thought of sausages again today. Ellen was obviously not very keen, either.

Then Henning caught her by the hair and heaved until

91

she got up. Chris clenched his fists in his pockets. What a brute!

He did not know that he had spoken aloud.

'Well, yes, but she's so lazy,' whispered Rasmus apologetically.

'I don't give a hang! Does *your* father yank your mother up by the hair if she doesn't do what he says at once?'

Rasmus gave him a furious look.

'Rasmus, now that they're on their feet, ask them if they've got a transistor you can borrow. Say I'm boring the ears off you and you want some music!'

'Okay.'

Chris watched tensely. Henning waved his hands about and shrugged his shoulders, but finally went to look for one. Or at least, he followed Ellen out of the room.

It was some time before he came back, and when he did, he was holding a transistor. He beckoned to Rasmus, who went over and got it. Almost before Rasmus had it in his hands, Henning had turned to Carl:

'Carl, you must help me over to the other wing with Henrik. They left town by car an hour and a half ago, so they may be here soon. Ellen has gone for coffee and food – I hope the cow doesn't smash the car up. Viggo, Mick, can you pull yourselves together, or perhaps you'd better go with Henrik – I don't want any fuss. One of you ought perhaps to stay with him, in any case,' he added, 'he's a bit too high for my liking.'

Carl raised himself laboriously from the mattress. 'Take it easy, Henning,' he said in his booming voice. 'Your artistic temperament is running away with you! We'll make it, all right. Are there any developments?'

Henning began to pull Henrik to his feet. 'I don't know – we agreed to be careful about the telephone, just in case. Those devils have ears everywhere. But Yutta and

Torben are on their way, and Pierre is driving, so it should be quick – the Gallic temperament, you know?' He giggled nervously.

Chris and Rasmus looked at each other and switched on the radio as if by silent agreement.

The newsreader on the twelve o'clock bulletin said that there was 'no news, in the search for the Prime Minister's son. All available police are involved but for the time being there is no news, and nothing has been heard from the kidnappers.' And then he said that everyone in the country should help by looking in their own cellars and attics.

'That wasn't much,' said Rasmus discontentedly. 'You'd think they could find us, with all that spying equipment they have . . .'

Chris said that they certainly were not going to tell everything they knew and risk warning the criminals.

He should not have said that. Rasmus went completely berserk and began all over again from the beginning, about capitalist lackeys and imperialist aggressors and social justice and the universities and the rent and the PLO and the Blacks.

Chris let him talk and in the end he paused to draw breath.

'Do shut up, Rasmus! I'm sorry I said criminals, I didn't mean your father. And I've never said that there are not masses of things which need dealing with, I know that from my father. He's always impatient, because one can't get things done at once, even when they're good things. But first you have to make sure that the changes aren't going to bring something worse, because everything hangs together. So it all takes far too long. I just think it's a waste of time to talk about it, when you're our age and don't know enough. All we can do is repeat what the adults say, the ones we know and who we know mean

93

well. We don't even know who is right, do we? We just *think* one or the other is.'

'You have to have a point of view!' said Rasmus hotly. 'It's zombies like you who ruin everything.'

'*I* haven't ruined anything. And I don't want to make up "points of view" about things I know nothing about, apart from what other people say. I want proof, not opinions!' Chris yawned. 'But since you're so keen on them, I'll gladly give you a viewpoint about one thing I *do* know: there is nothing in the world which is so right that it is right to use force to get it! And you can talk yourself blue in the face, but you won't move me from that. Why don't we shut up for now, so that we don't miss anything, if Torben and the others come up here?'

Rasmus gave him a look of contempt and switched to Denmark with a great deal of noise, and Chris fetched the chessboard.

Ellen came back. She had combed her hair and put on a little lipstick and she put some water on the hot-plate before starting to clear the things out of the 'larder'. Henning and Carl had returned as well, and a little later Viggo came in with Torben, the 'female' and Pierre.

Chris looked away quickly, but shook Rasmus stealthily by the arm. 'See if you can hear what they're talking about,' he whispered. 'Remember that you don't know you've been kidnapped!'

Rasmus got up without speaking and crossed the room.

I could have tried to go with him, of course, thought Chris, but if they're going to discuss any bright ideas, they would only chase me away again. If I look sufficiently absorbed in my chess, they may not remember to talk so quietly.

He listened as hard as he could, but without much success. It was such a long, low room that you heard only fragments of a sentence, a word here and there.

94

Rasmus came back, holding a cup carefully.

'Coffee, here you are, milk, oranges – the rolls are good.'

'What are they talking about?'

'Arguing about what to do. The people are furious about this business with you. There's talk of a demonstration.'

Chris took the orange. 'Get back there quickly. They mustn't suspect.'

What demonstration? Chris bit hungrily into a roll. The coffee was almost too strong, but it was good to get something different from the endless orange juice. They surely must see for themselves that the only thing to do was to send him home; after all, they weren't all out of their minds, there must be some law students among these activists? It was all very fine to say that you didn't respect Parliament or the law or anything, but that was just rubbish, none of those things collapsed just because someone said they didn't respect them. And when they realized that they could not achieve anything by it, they couldn't keep him in this attic for ever. You couldn't bury a boy alive, not in Denmark, the country was much too small, luckily.

Not *alive*. Chris's thoughts stood still for a moment; then he drew a breath of relief.

Thank God he had not said, even to Rasmus, that he knew where he was! They didn't have to be afraid of sending him home, or perhaps driving him somewhere and putting him down. He could only repeat a few first names, or so they thought, and those were not necessarily the real ones.

If Henning knew that I could tell . . .

Calm down, now! Chris told himself. He must be mentally ill in some way – I'm sure he is. He's a coward too, and it's the cowardly bullies who are the most

95

dangerous. But the others are there too, and no one knows that I know anything . . .

Torben got up and came towards him, and at that moment Chris remembered that he still had the Møllers' name and address written on a piece of lavatory paper in his pocket.

7

For a moment he was so frightened that he simply did not hear what Torben was saying, there was such a ringing in his ears. But after all, why should they suddenly take it into their heads to search him?

'. . . but you yourself must realize by now that the police are not going to find you and that there's no question of our sending you home. So get going, you, and try to convince your father! You can write what you like. You obviously know that you mustn't say anything that doesn't suit us.'

Chris got up. 'What do you want?' he said. 'I can't say I'm not being fed, can I? Even if I am pretty tired of eating sausages all the time. But perhaps *you* would prefer me to say that I'm getting nothing to eat?'

'You little shit – this isn't a novel, it's deadly earnest! You can leave the literature to your father and the other tools of the system. Just write what you know to be true. Tell them you haven't a chance of escaping; otherwise write what you like, but don't make it too long, we're in a hurry.'

Chris hesitated for a moment.

'Do get on, Christopher! This isn't a trap. We can't play any tricks with your scribble, can we? And I'm sure your mother will be glad to hear from you.'

Somehow he seemed to be looking much older, even since last Thursday, thought Chris. Could he be beginning to realize that they were never going to get anything out of this situation?

It did not take long to write. He had been thinking it over for several days, trying to work out how to provide a clue if he were given permission to write home, or actually ordered to do so.

'Dear Father and Mother, I have been told to write to you. I expect you will be glad to hear from me, too, so I thought I might as well do it. I don't know where I am, because I was blindfolded when I got here, but I can't escape because there are a lot of people on guard here and only one door – locked, of course – and it's too high for me to jump out of the window. I hope you don't think I'm an awful idiot. I went with them willingly because the man said you were going to have supper at his house and he seemed quite ordinary.

It's no good writing down names, because even if I was allowed to, they're probably really called something quite different. I *have* tried to explain that Father can't suddenly go and withdraw us from NATO, even if he wanted to, but they don't believe it. Or rather, they don't really listen. You know the kind of people who are dead certain they are the only ones who are right, so they think it's a waste of time listening to what other people think.

Otherwise I'm all right; it's just boring being indoors all day long when you're not ill. But they have

97

a radio and television and they have lent me a chessboard – a funny one, because although white is more or less white, black is completely green! Oh well, it doesn't matter. I wish I had a change of clothes, and I hope Mother doesn't give me sausages when I get home! But otherwise I'm all right, and I'm not particularly miserable, just cross.

With love to you and to Jørgen,

Chris.'

What a lot of idiots they were! The letter had to go the rounds, of course, and they at once started arguing about whether they would let him write 'offensively' about their 'debating technique', and whether it was sensible to let him say that he was not on the ground floor. The female translated the contents for Pierre and that at least showed that it mattered what Pierre thought. What he said – said the female – was that it was a poor cause that could not take criticism from 'the careerist brood' who did not understand a word of the movement's high aims; and the clearer it was that the letter was genuine and written voluntarily, the better.

So the outcome was that it should go off as it was.

Chris yawned with sheer relief. Carl had of course said something about 'it's deplorable that a child should already be so hardened that he had nothing in his head besides the playthings of a vanished age, made for the parasites on the working people, in a situation where he, despite his youth, could have contributed to the communication of the truth to a misled and exploited population'.

He had obviously never set foot in a chess club, if that was his view of chess! Chris's own toughest opponent was an apprentice plumber. As if everyone didn't have work to do, anyway! Carl was a real snob. Father had once said

98

that when people used the expression 'the working people' you could be absolutely certain that they did not count themselves as one of them. They were just pretending, in a condescending way.

Condescending – that was just what Carl was, and so damn' pleased with himself and his long, affected sentences that he didn't take a blind bit of notice of other people. That applied to the whole lot of them, of course. Not one of them had smelled a rat. Perhaps that was a little unjust – after all, the others couldn't know that both he and Father and Mother knew that chess set, and its rarity and value.

Chris was suddenly seized by doubt: he had not dared to describe it clearly. First they would get the letter – but who was going to deliver it? Torben and the others had gone again; perhaps they would drop it in on the police, or something. Jørgen would certainly have gone home, so they would all read it together once, and then again, and he had actually given details of all the kinds of things grown-ups ask about: food and clean underclothes and so on. And then one of them would say: 'What does he mean about the chess set?' At home they knew quite well that he was not a zombie! And then they would think of Baron Corfeldt.

Cripes, it was going to be wonderful to see the gangs' faces when the police suddenly turned up here! Perhaps they could be here by this evening?

Calm down now, Chris told himself, you can't be sure that it will be this evening, it depends how many detours they make with the letter. And if you don't watch out they may get suspicious. Not the others, but that Henning. He mustn't discover that I'm suddenly feeling cheerful.

Rasmus. If only there were some way of preventing anyone from knowing that Rasmus had been here too. Mr and Mrs Møller were too good to be involved in this kind of muck, so what good would it do for Mr Møller to go to prison, and Mrs Møller too, perhaps, so that there was no one to look after Tina? Quite apart from the fact that it would make Rasmus so wild that there would be no hope of talking sense to him!

And that is important, thought Chris. It's important that he doesn't start hating. They *hate* so much. You can't ever put the world right, simply by hating. If you hate someone, you don't think that anything they say can make sense. So you stop listening . . . so you can't talk to each other any more . . . and that's when you start fighting. I mustn't hate.

It was very quiet, now that Torben and the others had gone. Henrik was still with Mick somewhere else in the house, and Henning and Carl had not come back yet. Viggo was writing something at a table beside the cupboard with the kitchen things in it and Ellen was just lying on a mattress, smoking cigarettes and gazing up into the air.

Rasmus was staring out of their own window.

'It will be dark again soon, won't it?' Chris stood beside him.

'Where the devil are we? This is the most deadly hole . . .'

'That's only because you don't know it,' said Chris soothingly. 'It's the same when you look out of the windows of your own house. It's nearly winter, after all: windy and wet and cold, no leaves on the trees. It must be pretty here in summertime.'

It *was*, but there was no need to tell Rasmus that he knew that. It would not help, and what Rasmus did not know he could not blurt out.

'You get so ruddy confused, staying indoors all the time,' Rasmus complained, 'but perhaps you don't mind?'

'I do, but it's no use grumbling about things you can't

do anything about,' said Chris quietly, and Rasmus said 'Zombie', almost as a matter of form.

'I pinched Yutta's lighter,' he added.

'Great! Why her, though?'

'Argh – I don't know. Well, it was just lying there in her bag. The men's are in their pockets, not so easy to get at.'

It sounded as if this was not the real explanation, or not the only one. Perhaps Rasmus couldn't stand her either? But there was no point in talking about it. Rasmus would undoubtedly feel compelled to defend her, because it was one thing to be angry with her and the others because they had cheated his father, but it was asking too much for him to realize that Mr Møller and the others probably didn't even hold the same views.

Instead, Chris said: 'Look, when they come for us – if we're lucky, I mean, and someone sees you signalling – it would be better for you to hide. You can always get yourself home afterwards.'

'Why the hell?' Rasmus was suspicious at once.

'To keep your father and mother out of it, you fool! If I don't give it away that I haven't been here all the time, it will be just a private matter between your father and the others, and as soon as I'm free they won't get anything out of keeping you, will they? So they can just drive you home.'

'Why should you do that?'

He really was an unbearable fellow!

'Why shouldn't I?'

Rasmus stalled and muttered something about 'revenge', and Chris clenched his fists in his pockets and warned himself to take it easy.

'Do you really think of nothing but violence and hatred and revenge and "you hit me first"?' he said. 'You know, that revolting world you're trying to make – it's not one

101

I want to live in! Do you have to have everything put up in lights? Okay: I have nothing against your father and mother – well, a little against your father, perhaps, but not much. If he goes to prison it's you and your mother and Tina who will suffer – and what am I supposed to revenge myself for? I'm not particularly bothered about revenge. I don't think it gives you any satisfaction – you just have a flat, empty feeling afterwards. I'm not even bothered about revenging myself on Torben and the others here, I just look forward to getting away from all their hatred, but I don't want to protect them, because I think they're dangerous to other people and they have to be stopped – particularly her, Yutta, and the one you call Henning.'

'Oh, Henning's just a crazy shit,' said Rasmus uncertainly.

Chris got off the bed again. 'Is he?' he said seriously. 'Have you ever looked at him, properly? Have you seen the way he smiles? And his eyes, which jump from one person to another as if they have no connection with what he is saying? I think he's crazy too, but I think he's crazy in earnest. And I think he's evil.'

'Well, yes, I'm not specially keen on him,' said Rasmus sullenly, regarding the tips of his shoes with attention. 'But evil – what do you mean by that? That's cra-um-crazy talk.'

Chris sighed. It wasn't easy to talk when you didn't even know the same words.

'I don't think you can mean many things by "evil",' he said patiently. 'But I can give you an example: for instance, I think that even if I don't say anything about your father and mother and you, it may not do any good, because Henning might easily grass about them just because he likes hurting people.' Rasmus flipped the transistor antenna thoughtfully. 'That would be just like

102

him,' he said. 'Mum can't stand him either. But he's one of ours, politically, I mean.'

Chris was about to say that you should take better care what company you kept, but he gave it up. It wasn't always necessary to have the last word, and Rasmus' eyes were worried. It was better for him to start thinking for himself a bit rather than to keep on rubbing things in.

'It's just on four o'clock,' he said instead.

There was no news on the radio this time, just something about the university and the usual students who were annoyed about something or other, but everyone was used to that.

The afternoon dragged for Chris. Henning and Carl came back and Mick came shuffling in too, with Henrik; he had to be half carried, because he had just been sick. Then they all settled down again in their circle on the mattresses. The candles were lighted. Carl began to drone away. He always talked as though he had a potato in his mouth.

Chris had never gone in for having nightmares, as far as he could remember. There must be something about this loft, he thought. I feel as if I've been here for ever, it is as if time stood still, as if there were no difference between night and day, except for the little bit of light in the middle of the day; as if it were the same day, going on and on, as if nothing else could ever happen. It feels as if I couldn't possibly ever become Chris again; I'm just an object, up in a loft, among the other objects in a loft.

Chris sat on the rocking-horse and rocked to and fro. He even smiled a little; he had probably got up with the vague idea of preventing the dust from covering him completely in greyness – as long as you moved, at least you couldn't get dusty! That was all nonsense, of course, but you got quite peculiar, just sitting and sitting and sitting.

103

'What the hell, you swine! You don't have to vomit over the rest of us. Damn you to hell!'

The voice split the long room, Henning's high, flat voice. It was Henrik who was in trouble again, vomiting and vomiting, while Henning jumped up in a state of hysteria and rushed off for some paper to wipe his shoes.

Carl shook his head and stopped talking for a moment, long enough to move his mattress a little further towards the middle of the loft. Then he went back and fetched the tray with all the lighted candles on it and put them in front of him. Mick followed with the second mattress and Ellen began to shout: 'I'm damn well not going to wipe up after that idiot!' Mick came over and fetched a newspaper or two. Rasmus and Chris both looked enquiringly at him, but he merely shrugged his shoulders and made an indifferent grimace before going back to spread them over the floor where Henrik had been sick.

'They can't just leave it there!' Chris burst out angrily. 'We soon won't be able to breathe for the stink in this room!'

Viggo was holding Henrik by the arm. 'Leave it off, Henrik,' was all he said. 'Stop it now, can't you?'

As if anyone vomited if they could possibly help it! Chris and Rasmus looked irresolutely at each other. 'There must at least be a bucket somewhere,' said Chris with sudden determination. 'Come on!'

They found two soup-plates, and by their joint efforts Henrik was moved across the mattress a little, so that his head was on the other side. 'Lift his head a bit and hold him round the forehead.' Chris pushed one plate under Henrik's cheek. 'Don't let go, or he'll get his whole face in it!'

'He's damn well done that already,' said Rasmus furiously.

Chris knew that, and had a bad conscience about

104

leaving the worst job to Rasmus; but if he had touched it himself he would simply have been sick too.

A kitchen roll – surely even a slut like Ellen must have a kitchen roll somewhere? There it was. Chris went back and wiped the worst of the mess off Henrik's face; then he dipped a fresh piece in water and wiped again.

He and Rasmus looked at each other without speaking. Viggo had gone off to join the others as soon as the boys arrived. Carl was talking again. From time to time they could hear Henning's voice, and Mick and Viggo were both talking at once, which made Ellen giggle.

Chris looked across at them and back at Rasmus, who had been doing the same thing. 'Give me some paper too,' said Rasmus shortly. His voice was shaking a little.

'There's some water over there. I'll hold him now while . . .' Chris handed a long strip of paper to Rasmus and put a doubled piece over his own hand before holding Henrik's forehead.

The young man tried to shake his head and free himself, but he had no more strength than an infant. Chris held his breath as he pushed the dirty plate away and wedged the other in its place.

Soon there was nothing more coming up, but Henrik went on groaning and whimpering.

'Shall I put you down?' asked Chris in a low voice. Henrik merely groaned again and Chris gently put his head back on the mattress. The dreadful noise made you feel quite desperate inside; it sounded like an animal to which something horrible had been done.

'And they don't care!' he whispered to Rasmus, who was standing beside him now and listening too. 'They wouldn't dream of lifting a finger, the . . . the loathsome, low animals!'

Rasmus suggested quietly that they might get a clean mattress and try to roll him over onto it.

It was rather like trying to handle a rag-doll, except that a rag-doll never made those ghastly sounds. Soon afterwards they became fainter.

'He's freezing!' said Chris. 'Look, he's beginning to shiver!'

Henrik had not so much as opened his eyes once. When Rasmus asked him if he was cold, he opened them, but they did not focus and he closed them again without answering.

As if by common agreement, Chris and Rasmus each took a corner of the mattress and pulled it like a sledge up to their own end, with the blue lamp and the peculiar sofa. Neither of them looked at any of the others as they passed and Chris went back past them to get a blanket as if he didn't know they were there.

'Now he's sweating!' Rasmus protested, when he came back with the blanket.

Chris put it carefully over the young man. 'Perhaps he's getting a fever,' he said. 'He may be cold again in a minute.'

He was. He shivered so hard that his whole body jerked and the teeth chattered loudly in his head.

Chris and Rasmus were so busy looking after him that they had not heard anyone crossing the room. 'Aha, I see the local Red Cross is on the job.' Henning's flat voice was indifferent, almost amused, and his eyes were quite expressionless as he glanced down at Henrik before walking away again.

Rasmus muttered a very long string of the most indecent swear words under his breath and for once Chris felt no urge to protest.

They sat in silence for a little, one on each side of Henrik's mattress. Suddenly he began to weep loudly. Chris was quite stiff and empty inside with discomfort and despair; it was Rasmus who leaned close and whis-

106

pered in a muffled voice: 'Don't you worry, Henrik, me and Chris will look after you.'

But there's nothing to look after, thought Chris wretchedly. He should have been a young man, quick and full of fun, doing all manner of things, and he's turned himself into nothing, just a sick lump of flesh you don't know what to do with. Hasn't he even got a father and mother to help him?

The same question burst from him when Carl came over a little later. The older man shook his head: 'There's nothing they can do, my lad. They try, every time they find him, but he runs away from them again. He shouldn't have got on to the hard stuff, he should have stuck to hash, but you need character for that.'

'You might use character for keeping off hash as well,' Chris snapped. 'It seems a more sensible idea! But of course that will turn out to be just another Imperialist view!'

Carl was not even angry. 'Certainly not, my boy. You must take care not to confuse the different concepts; we are not supporters of drugs, as such. But there are always weaker souls, they need something, too. And if they only stick to hash, there is no great harm done.

'Now come over and have something to eat, boys. There's nothing you can do for him, and he will be feeling better soon. We're used to his turns. Ellen has made *boeuf Stroganov* and Torben has brought you a fresh supply of orange juice.'

The boys got up reluctantly and prepared to follow him.

'I'm damned if I feel particularly hungry after all that,' said Rasmus. 'How about you?'

Chris yawned long and loud. If he had believed that Rasmus understood the words 'pitiless' and 'ruthless', he would have said that he had never met anyone they suited as well as Carl! But there was no point in saying so.

'I can't stand the way he said that,' said Rasmus angrily, following Chris's example by running a comb through his hair. 'That about the weaker souls, I mean. It can't be right that just because people are not much use to society, you can give them that poisonous rubbish . . . He can't have meant it the way he said it.'

Chris did not answer. Rasmus would know quite well what he was thinking. 'To table, man!' he said.

'What about the morse? I haven't managed to do anything, because of all that business with Henrik.'

Chris said it would have to wait, because at this hour everyone would be indoors for supper.

Nor was it even necessary now, because the police would be able to drive straight here, but of course Rasmus didn't know that.

It was quite simple to produce *boeuf Stroganov* when you only had to tip it out of a tin; she didn't even taste it to see if it needed a little seasoning!

I mustn't be so fussy, thought Chris, ashamed; at least it's clean and there must be some kind of nourishment in it. Lots of people in the world would be able to survive if only they had a tin of *Stroganov* which tasted like nothing at all.

On the other hand, it wasn't so good when you were used to food tasting nice, because your mother took trouble over it. It didn't actually help anyone in the developing countries if you didn't bother to make the food taste good in Denmark, since it was the Danes who were eating it anyway.

'Isn't Henrik going to have any?' he asked aloud, as Henning scraped the last morsels from the pan.

Carl said he could never eat anything when he was like this, and Rasmus added a warning that it would only come up again. Chris had really only said it because Henning was scraping out the pan without so much as asking the others if they would like any more.

'Well, if they did they could say so,' said Rasmus casually, when Chris mentioned it later.

The seven o'clock news bulletin said that the Minister of Justice was going to make a statement about the kidnapping on television news.

'I had better do some morse beforehand,' whispered Rasmus. 'Otherwise people will be indoors again, watching.'

'Okay. If you can get to it, try the other door over there.'

Rasmus scowled. 'I've done that already,' he muttered. 'This morning. It wasn't too damn nice here this morning, while you were asleep. I would have liked to go for a walk, but that damn door is locked too.'

Chris had not dared to hope otherwise, but it would have been silly not to try. The way they slopped around here, especially as soon as Torben and the female had gone, someone *might* have forgotten it.

What was the Minister going to say? They could not possibly be so stupid as to reveal that they had a clue, but it seemed to Chris that the next twenty minutes passed at a snail's pace. He could not even concentrate on the chess board. Rasmus came back and whispered glumly that there was nothing but darkness in all directions, however often he flicked the lighter on and off.

Chris consoled him that that was just why someone *might* have seen it, and people didn't always go round with a torch in their pockets to reply to morse signals! Rasmus cheered up a bit and Chris suddenly caught himself having quite a big-brotherly feeling for him. How on earth did a boy like that get along in ordinary life?

I ought not to be so jolly smug, Chris reminded himself.

In the first place, I've got a much more sensible father and mother and a big brother, too, and in the second place I'm a bit of an idle hound, I know that, even if it irritates me when Mother says so. I simply don't want to get myself worked up over everything.

But I shall never be quite so idle again. Not that I want to start getting mixed up in all sorts of things I don't understand. But I shall never again get out of it by saying that the worst things are too far away for me to bother about. They're not. Well, perhaps the very worst are, but evil things can happen here in Denmark, too. Where there are people who are evil, like Henning and that female, evil can happen. And they can always find people who are too hot-headed and stupid to see what they are getting mixed up in.

You have to be on your guard. There's not much a boy can do, of course, not the kind of heroic things that Rasmus dreams about. But you can watch out and not let yourself be talked round. I'm going to listen to what people say and then I'm going to watch what they *do*. It's so easy to say something which sounds good, but it's more difficult – and more important – to *do* something good.

If I had had time, I would have tried to explain it to Rasmus, so that he would never let himself be taken in again by smart talk about a better society from a revolting hooligan like that Henning, who pulls his wife's hair and doesn't lift a finger to help anyone.

But luckily the police were bound to come soon! Chris got up and followed Rasmus over to the television.

8

The announcer was reading out his letter! Crikey, how embarrassing it sounded, being read out like that, to everyone in the country! A new thought occurred to him, with real terror this time: what if he read the bit about the chess set aloud?

Phoo! He had stopped, just before the part about the radio and television and chess. Chris's diaphragm sank back into its place again; everything sounded so significant when it was read out in an announcer's voice.

Chris listened with only half an ear as the usual things were said about there unfortunately being no trace of the culprits as yet.

'Aren't you glad about my aristocratic connections, my friends?' said Henning hatefully, over the announcer's voice. Carl said quickly: 'Hold your tongue, Henning!' with a side-long look at Chris, who had fortunately put on a sleepy expression as soon as the letter began.

As usual, Rasmus noticed nothing. Well, even if he had asked what Henning meant, it would not have mattered, after Henning had been warned. But once again Chris was glad that he had not told Rasmus what he knew. It would have been just like him to say 'Oh, do you mean Baron Corfeldt?'

Of course, the situation wasn't dangerous . . . now. For the hundred-and-seventeenth time, Chris took hold of the little gnawing fear somewhere in the back of his mind and pushed it further away. But it was really just as well that Henning did not know that *he* knew where he was, as long as he was still there.

Then the Minister read out something about criminal law, about kidnappers and how long you went to prison for kidnapping. He announced that the kidnappers would be given a safe conduct, and all police would be withdrawn from Chris's home until twelve o'clock tomorrow morning, in an attempt to deal with this 'highly deplorable and foolish action' before it 'brought lasting harm to young hotheads who must long ago have reached the conclusion that their action was senseless.'

Chris wondered anxiously for a moment about the safe conduct, but only for a moment. On the contrary, it was very clever: like this, no one would suspect that they were already on their way here.

For surely they must be? Father and mother could not possibly be so overcome that they had simply not noticed the information?

'Reports have been circulating in one or two papers,' said the announcer, 'that the Prime Minister intended to resign, or that the Government was thinking of handing in its resignation. Prime Minister Egstrup has not been available for interview, but Television News has the Prime Minister's eldest son, Jørgen Egstrup, a law student, in the studio.'

Chris clenched his hands in his pockets and swallowed back a yawn. It was a bit thick that his own elder brother was forced to get up there and talk to a person like Henning! Jørgen was wearing a navy-blue sweater knitted by their aunt; a lock of hair was falling into his eyes as usual.

A woman interviewer asked Jørgen if he knew anything about the rumours and Jørgen said politely that he did not, because he seldom had time to read more than the morning papers.

But did he know anything about his father's plans?

Jørgen smiled politely again and said that at all events his father was not planning to resign and take the whole Government with him, in order to revenge himself on the electors and Parliament! *They* were not the ones who had done anything.

'But perhaps your father would like more freedom of action?'

'As far as I can tell from my studies, the Prime Minister has the same right as other citizens in Denmark to ask the police to search for minors who have been removed from their homes by deception or force and held against their will. He does not need any more freedom than he has, and I cannot see that it has anything to do with the case whether it is his own child or someone else's.'

Chris had never thought before about how handsome Jørgen was. And he was neither excited nor embarrassed, nor upset in any obvious way. He just answered calmly, politely and clearly. But he *was* worked up, really: the vein on his temple was jumping, just as Father's did when he was keeping back a yawn.

Then the interviewer presumed his father and mother must of course have been pleased to get a letter from Chris, and Jørgen said: 'Of course.'

And when Jørgen's face looked like that, a little distant and vague, one didn't ask any more questions along those lines, Chris thought warningly, but of course the interviewer could not know that, so she said – it was very sweet of her, in a way – 'Christopher also said in his letter that he was allowed to listen to radio and watch television: wouldn't you like to say a few words to him?'

Jørgen gave that polite smile again, but he looked stern. 'No thanks. It is kind of you, but Chris knows very

113

well that we care, at home, and I don't think he would much like being talked to in public. That can wait until he comes home.'

Certainly none of the others would have seen it, but Chris's eyes were glued to the screen, hoping for – he didn't know what. And as Jørgen turned away he sent a little smile over his shoulder and took his hand out of his pocket. In his hand was a pawn. One second, and it was gone.

So they could be here at any moment. It had been difficult enough up to now to conceal the fact that he was downright wretched, but it was even more difficult to conceal the fact that he was bubbling with expectation. Chris yawned and yawned, until at last Rasmus said irritably that he couldn't possibly be quite so sleepy at that hour, when he had slept till half-past ten that morning.

At last – at last! A car crackled up to the door below and stopped with a screech of brakes. Viggo rose from his mattress and went to unlock the door and Chris and Rasmus looked out of their own window. There were two cars – would there be a fight? Chris thought anxiously. It looks as if they must be prepared for one, coming in two cars like that.

He could see them now, in the light from the door which Viggo had gone down to open. Why were they not police cars? Proper police cars, painted white, with a light on top?

Rasmus turned away, but Chris stayed at the window, looking out but unable to see anything. He had an extraordinarily stupid, buzzing sensation in his head. Excited voices came from a long way off – Torben's – the female's . . .

It was not the police.

He blinked three or four times to clear his vision again

and squeezed his hands together hard behind his back. If he was going to think, he had better think fast now. Even before Torben spoke, Chris knew what he was going to say:

'We've got to get out, quickly! Viggo and Mick, drag Henrik down to the car, we can't leave him behind here. The rest of you, pack up, everything's got to go, all your things. If they are thorough enough they will be able to see that someone has been here, but there must be nothing to show them *who*. We've got ten minutes – a quarter of an hour, at most!'

Even the female helped. The food cupboard was cleared out, the mattresses set on end against the walls. Carl brought a couple of paper-bags and everything was thrown in, candles, clothes, all higgledy-piggledy.

'What has happened?' asked Henning. His voice sounded different, less affected, but frightened.

'They're on their way here – someone must have talked too much, or else you've been careless.'

Henning interrupted shrilly: 'That's a lie! I'm living here quite openly! It was the perfect place, who the hell would have suspected that old idiot?'

'There's no time for talk,' said the female sharply. 'You may have bought too many supplies, but it doesn't matter what has happened, we just have to get out. The last time we picked them up on the radio they were on their way – not more than fifteen miles off.'

'What did they know? Apart from the place, I mean?' Carl's voice was not as booming as usual, but that was probably because he was messing about trying to get the electric hotplates into a bag which was too small for them.

'Take the plates as they are! I don't think they know any more than that, but that, at least, they seem to be quite certain of. Pierre advised us not to tune in again.'

'Do you mean that those swine might have found *your* radio?' Henning burst out incredulously. 'Fixed it, or whatever it's called – I've never given any thought to those tiresome technical things.'

At any other time Chris would have been doubled up with laughter, but this time he did not even smile over the 'cheek' of the police.

Rasmus had begun to roll his sleeping-bag up slowly. Chris realized that what he was squeezing in his hand was one of the chessmen. He stuck it hastily in his pocket and began to roll up his sleeping-bag too. There were the dirty socks, the ones he had been wearing that evening, so long ago. He covertly stuffed one in his pocket; how much time would they have to check up? For safety's sake he rolled the other up as mother rolled up clean socks and put his handkerchief inside so that it looked fat enough.

The idea was only a tiny beginning, and there might be no chance, but one could try.

'If you want to go to the lavatory, go now,' Torben called up to them. 'We'll be leaving in a moment.'

'And pack up those blasted chess pieces, boy!' added Henning. 'I don't want any mess!'

Chris obeyed, remembering at the last moment to take one from the white set as well. None of them knew anything about chess; there was a good chance that they didn't know if there should be fifteen or sixteen of each colour, but if there were fifteen of one and sixteen of another . . .

Perhaps they simply would not have time to come back and make sure that he had not forgotten anything, but it was better to think of everything.

'Wouldn't it be more sensible for me to stay?' Henning's voice was suddenly smooth and ingratiating. 'Not up here, of course, but downstairs, with my paints and easel, where I have every right to be this winter. Don't forget the old trick, Yutta, it's best to hide something where people have already looked – I might be more use if I stayed.'

Yutta did not even look at him. 'We can't do without you. There has to be someone to look after the blasted boy, doesn't there? We can't involve any more people in it at this point, it's too risky.'

Pierre brushed the dust off his hands and said something, probably asking what Henning had said, because afterwards Yutta said that he had agreed with her.

If only he could have written a message, it would have been safer – behind the rocking-horse, for instance. Father and mother knew that he had seen that before. But there were too many for him to risk it; they were in a tremendous hurry, but there was always one of them close by. And before you could get out a biro – and there were five letters in 'Chris' – no, they couldn't help seeing, it was better not to try.

Rasmus had not said a word since the others arrived. He was looking bitter and he kept on stopping and gnawing his thumb-nail. That usually meant that he was really trying to think.

'Right then, we can have the lights off, can't we?' said Torben, looking round. 'What about the boys? Christopher, I mean – is there any point in all that business of blindfolding him?'

Yutta picked up her bag and looked irritably at Chris and Rasmus. Chris yawned and Rasmus said angrily: 'Oh, drop it!'

She took no notice of that, naturally, 'No,' she said, after thinking it over. 'We are late. We'll go downstairs by torchlight and it's no good trying to guide them down at speed if they can't see where they're going. It's so dark

117

that it won't make any difference – later, when we get to our destination, we'll blindfold them.'

It was a help that the only light was from torches, but it would still be difficult enough. Chris took the steps in double time, making sure that he stayed beside Carl, while he worked feverishly in his pocket to get the chessman into the sock. Carl was holding his arm as he had been told to, but he was quite middle-aged, so he had enough trouble getting down the stairs. In any case, he never thought about other people, only about how he sounded; it would not occur to him to wonder if someone else was planning anything.

If I gave a sudden jerk, thought Chris, he would fall, and let go of me to use both his hands. I know how to fall without hurting myself, but is there any chance? The door is straight ahead down there . . .

He did not dare. Pierre, Viggo and Henning were all ahead of him and just behind came Torben with Rasmus. And to cap it all, there was Mick down there with Henrik. No, it would be stupid, it would be sheer accident if things went well, and afterwards, if he failed, *they* would be much more on their guard.

There had been a crackle on the drive when the cars arrived. If only it were raining, he could take special care to plant his feet firmly and leave some good tracks. If the other didn't succeed, that was the only thing left to do.

'Look, Torben, we are a hell of a crowd for two cars! If you give me money for the ticket, I could take the train.'

That was very neatly done! Chris knew the difference now from Rasmus' genuine voice, but Torben certainly didn't. So that was the plan Rasmus had been chewing over. If only it didn't make them suspicious!

But all Torben said was: 'That won't do, Ras; it's a long way to the railway station and we have no time to plan it. They must be right on our heels. It'll be all right, even if it's a bit tight.'

They were almost down now. Now was the moment to keep a clear head; what could he afford to let them see? Not the knife, not the watch with the compass on it – one of the marbles? Yes, one of the marbles! Only Rasmus could possibly know that they were not his own.

The air was sharp. That meant that it was the frost that had made the cars crackle as they arrived. So there would not even be footprints.

He *must* succeed.

Chris's fingers gripped the marble. First, get out of the beam of light from the door, if they suddenly switched it on . . . and not just by the second car – *here*!

Chris turned his ankle over and let go of the marble at the same time, while Carl's grip tightened on his arm.

'Oof! I nearly fell then.'

'Well, look where you're going, boy!'

'I – I dropped a marble . . .'

Carl said nervously that they must leave it, they had no time. To hell with it, anyway! The marble was no use.

Fortunately Henning had been listening. 'I don't think it's a very good idea to leave His Excellency's property lying about, do you? So pick that marble up, my lad, and let's see a bit of cooperation.'

He had thrown it towards something darker in the darkness. It must be a bush, if he remembered rightly. There, a little to one side, where the headlamps would not catch it.

'Can you find it for yourself? These glasses of mine are no good for that kind of thing.' Carl was coming with him, still with a firm grip on his arm, while he looked anxiously down the long drive towards the road.

Now!

Chris leaned forward, laid the sock with the chessman

in the toe right at the edge of the shrubbery, took another step forward and picked up the marble. 'Here it is!' he said, with relief.

'Good, in with you then!'

It would be up to the police to find it, Chris told himself, trying to breathe normally again while his heart went on thumping hard. I couldn't put it any closer, but they *must* have some floodlights, they won't just go up and say: 'There's no one here. The Egstrups must have misunderstood.' They would have to search properly, and then they would find it, and mother would recognize the sock, it was the one with the candy-stripes which Jørgen had given him for his birthday.

They were almost at the end of the drive before he remembered the compass. He squeezed himself round a bit so that he could squint at it without anyone noticing. The compass was important now: the sock would give the police something to work on, but it might take time, and if he had some idea where he was, he would not feel quite so helpless.

Torben was driving. The same tradesman's van in which they had come here. Pierre sat on the front passenger seat. In the back, apart from Rasmus and himself, were Henrik and Mick. Henrik was sleeping in an extraordinarily noisy fashion, sometimes flinging out an arm or a leg; Mick was leaning against the back door, complaining that it was as cold as hell.

Torben fiddled with the instrument panel to turn the heat on and the van swerved a little.

'Drive careful!' said Pierre in his bad English.

'*Yes*, for God's sake! You don't think it would amuse me to be stopped, you idiot!'

'They will go there first and see that the bird has flown,' said Mick soothingly. 'They're damned unlikely to be bright enough to leave patrols behind them in advance – if you see what I mean.'

Torben said he hoped Mick was right.

Chris passionately hoped the opposite. He had not even thought of it, there had been so little time. At first he had believed that the police would be coming to get him, and later, when he realized they had been discovered, everything had moved so fast. It had been so vital to leave a clue, so that the police could see that father and mother had been right.

It's all the same really, Chris thought. I can't remember ever having been so horribly disappointed before in my life. If I had not had plenty to do I would have howled like a baby. And they're never going to have *that* satisfaction, he thought grimly.

Why shouldn't the police have put out patrols? Carl and the others always talked about them as if they were the most artful devils in the world, so they might easily work out that the criminals could tap their car radios.

But it would certainly not have occurred to them that their arrival would not be a complete surprise; what wretched bad luck that the female and Torben should have happened to hear them!

'Why the hell have you put the bars up, you shit?' asked Rasmus, suddenly and angrily from the darkness. 'Do you think we're a cageful of monkeys?'

Torben smiled at them in the driving mirror. 'Because of Henrik,' he said. 'If he wakes up properly there's a risk that he will begin to hit out and we don't want to land in the ditch, do we?'

'No-oh . . .'

There was a long silence. Then Rasmus tugged gently at Chris's arm and showed him that Mick was asleep. 'Shall we share an orange?' he said.

'Let's do that.'

You got used to the darkness; Chris could see Rasmus' face quite well. He was looking anxious, and he went on staring through the darkness at Chris, as if he were expecting something.

Then Pierre said something to Torben and Torben began to answer.

'Chris!' Rasmus whispered quickly. 'It was because I wanted to fetch my father that I said that about the train – so that he could get you out.'

Chris gave him a friendly nudge. 'Yes, I worked that one out,' he whispered back.

Now they were turning again. He put his hand out and showed Rasmus the compass. 'There are four pieces left to share,' he said, looking sternly at the other boy. Rasmus understood the signal and put up a triumphant thumb, and Chris hissed between his teeth: 'We're driving north.'

'Would you like some orange?'

Torben said he would and Rasmus stuffed the sections between the bars, and made some joke.

He was no fool. The more Torben and the others believed he was still on their side, the better.

But how much *was* he against them? Wasn't he the same as Mrs Møller: he objected to the means, not the end? He was against the female and the others because they had kidnapped him. Chris didn't blame him, because Rasmus and logic simply did not go together. He had wanted to slip home to his father and mother and get his father to release Chris. But was he also prepared to involve the police? If he was – if he could seize his chance to slip away as soon as the van stopped . . .

Chris remembered about the blindfold and sighed inwardly. How could one run with a blindfold on? Probably, *crash*, straight into a wall! The seconds it would take to pull the blindfold off if their hands were free would be too long. Torben and Pierre would be on top of them before they had moved five paces.

No matter how many ideas you had, there was a snag to every one of them. The same snag every time: the others were, quite simply, a superior force. It made no difference who was right, as long as there were enough on the side of the wrong. He thought he could have coped with one, whoever it was, but not several. And there were never less than three or four of them, except when they had a locked door to help them.

Both he and Rasmus jumped, and Mick woke up, when Torben switched on the car radio. The music positively crashed out before he switched to another station. Then there was nothing but a hissing sound.

'The hell with it,' he muttered. 'They've stopped using their radio.'

Mick straightened up and yawned. 'What did you expect? It's asking too much for them all to be mentally deficient. One of them must have had the brilliant idea that if the bird had flown, it could only be for one reason.'

'Yes, but how the devil am I to know if we're driving straight into their arms?'

Mick replied soothingly that 'the swine' would also be unable to keep an effective patrol going, and Torben admitted that there was something in that.

Perhaps this was a strange time to get frightened. After all, he had known almost from the beginning, that he *must* forget about it – it had stayed in the back of his mind and every time his thoughts had turned in that direction he had quickly pushed them another way.

Kidnappers sometimes killed their victims.

There was that Minister in Italy, and someone in Germany; and in South America . . . But one of them, in South America, had certainly helped to oppress the

123

population, hadn't he? Thrown them into prison, and treated them like Nazi guards in the old days?

It was no good. His heart was beginning to hammer and his mouth was filling with saliva. After all, these others had not done anything; they were meant to be merely hostages, and yet they had been murdered.

Calm down now! That was in Italy and Germany, after all. Here in Denmark all they did was to throw paving-stones about and destroy things and shout insults. They didn't do *that* kind of thing here, the other thing. They were all Danes, apart from Pierre; even Henning was a Dane.

It's also because they say 'swine'. Had they really never talked to a policeman? They were perfectly ordinary men, and sometimes young, too. Men whose work was to write parking tickets and catch thieves and stop men who were trying to kill their wives. All they were trying to do was to make people behave themselves, for the sake of those who had done nothing.

How must it feel to believe in something which made you think of a whole lot of people you didn't know as 'swine'? It must be frightening. It's frightening just to listen to – evil.

'I want a piss,' said Mick.

Torben exploded. 'Are you out of your mind, man? Here I am, driving around with the Prime Minister's son in the back, with all the fuzz in the country watching at every crossroads to catch us, and damn me to hell if you don't want a piss! You can bet on it I'm not going to stop this box until we're there, no matter what the hell you want!'

Chris grinned. Perhaps because he had been feeling so uncomfortable, and suddenly it all sounded like a silly film.

124

'Where are we going, Torben?' asked Rasmus in a casual tone.

'Copenhagen.'

Mick lighted a cigarette. 'Is that wise, Torben? Yutta . . .'

'Aahh, stuff it! As if the kids wouldn't be able to hear for themselves when we get to the town – if we get to it! Don't let's over-dramatize things more than necessary. Copenhagen is big enough; as long as they're blindfolded in good time it doesn't matter a damn, one way or the other.'

Chris and Rasmus looked at each other in the darkness and Chris slipped his watch carefully back into his pocket; to go by the bumps and the many bends in the road, Torben was keeping to country lanes all the time, but if they were going to land up in Copenhagen there was no need to keep an eye on the compass.

Torben and Pierre were talking again now; Pierre's English was poor, Torben's much better, even if it was not specially good. But if only they would keep it up, thought Chris; they don't expect Rasmus and me to understand them when they speak fast. In any case, Rasmus knows I'm bad at languages, he can tell them that if need be. None of them can possibly know I have an aunt in England and have been going there on holiday all my life. The fact that it doesn't sound right when I speak it is beside the point; at least I understand it!

If only they would say something useful, something which would give him information. But it was all just ordinary chat; Torben was asking about the student war there had been in France a few years ago and Pierre was telling him about it. Ah, now they were talking about someone called Wilfred who would be coming tomorrow, but since he didn't know who that was, it was neither here nor there.

Mick had just asked if Torben had the slightest idea where they were, when Henrik woke up. He sat up and hit his head on the roof of the car and began to shout and struggle so that Torben swerved. Mick got hold of him and said something soothing and Rasmus tried to help too, but Henrik seemed to become more and more uncontrollable.

'Give he somesing!' ordered Pierre in English.

Mick said that would be dangerous and tried once more to get Henrik to sit still, but it was no good. Rasmus tried to hold on to one arm, but Henrik was suddenly too strong for him. Chris held on to the other while Mick held him round the body. Henrik was unable to free the arm Chris was holding; Chris hoped inwardly that Mick was too busy to notice.

'You give he somesing!' In spite of the broken English, you could hear the threat in the voice.

'You'll damn well have to, Mick,' said Torben uneasily. 'I can't drive with him like this, he could cause an accident.'

Mick said he wasn't too keen on it. 'He's in an awful state – what if he snuffs it on us?'

'Give him a little, just enough so that you can hold him . . .'

Somehow they managed it. Mick promised him 'a shot', and sat on him, and Rasmus held Torben's lighter while Mick pushed the hypodermic into the arm Chris was holding.

'You're stronger than you look, aren't you?' said Mick.

Chris said there was nothing special about it, he had just happened to have the right hold.

He could hear his voice shaking, he had only just had the presence of mind to steer attention away from the kind of grip he was using. Was what he was doing right? Without his help Mick might not have managed to give

126

the injection – it was horrible to have helped to pump poison into somebody.

But they would not have been able to hold him, and at the speed Torben was driving they could have ended up in the ditch and all been killed. Nevertheless, it was horrible.

Henrik was beginning to calm down now; Mick stayed at his side and Rasmus crawled back until he was sitting beside Chris again. He said nothing, but sat chewing his thumb. A little later he shifted so that they were sitting close together.

'It's shitting cold here,' he said, in whispered apology. It was not particularly cold, not when you were sitting on sleeping-bags, and the heating was on, but inside you it felt cold, cold and black and sickening.

They drove some way in silence, interrupted only by Torben or Mick arguing from time to time as to which way they should take at the next turning. Then Pierre asked if Henrik was reliable. Torben said he had not always been like that, it was only recently that things had been so bad.

Pierre said almost apologetically that of course he did not mean to criticize and 'ze work could profit' from drug-users, 'but important *you* are one who has stuff! He depend on you, he do what you say. He get stuff self, you no have control! Zen he danger for work!'

'You're damned hard-boiled,' muttered Mick, and Torben said: 'That's not the way we do things. None of us have given Henrik more than a little bit of hash and we weren't the ones who taught him to use it. Henrik's in with us because he was a good chap and quite all right; he was a bit soft in the head, but he was just as keen on the work as the rest of us. We don't believe in the kind of approach you're talking about, it won't do for us.'

'Is he coming right out and recommending slave

labour?' asked Mick incredulously, in Danish. 'It sounded damn' like it.'

Rasmus asked anxiously: 'What were you talking about?'

Chris practically came out with the translation! Luckily he bit his tongue at the last moment and changed the word into a cough.

'Henrik,' said Torben. 'That it's a shame he's hooked.'

'He ought to go to hospital,' said Chris, as calmly as he could. 'I can't understand why you don't take him to hospital, Torben. I think he's very sick, and he can only be a burden to you.'

Torben sent a quick, wry smile into the driving mirror. 'Yes, but we can't risk letting him go now, can we? He might talk – after all, he knows *you* now. I don't know what kind of muck he's got hold of, he was smoking too much last time I saw him, but that was all. As soon as we can get him to a doctor, we'll do it. You mustn't think that we want that kind of thing going on.'

There was no harm in trying . . .

'What kind of thing *do* you want? I don't mean all that about Imperialism and profits and capitalist lackeys and so on, I understand that. But what is it you still want to use *me* for? Doesn't one of you know someone who knows enough to explain to you that what you want Father to do simply can't be done?'

'It's no damn' surprise that you'd like to get home, Christopher . . .'

Chris interrupted him. 'It's not that. Well, of course I want to, but it's not that; I just think it's absolutely crazy! You're not going to get anywhere. It would be much better to take up the safe conduct that Mr Petersen promised.'

'It's no good, Christopher. As long as we can use you

to put pressure on your father, we have to exploit that possibility. We'll achieve something, you wait!'

Chris sighed. 'Yes, but you could send Rasmus home, for heaven's sake. *He* can't stand *me*, and I wouldn't say he was my cup of tea, either, so why should we both miss school? He's stupid enough to begin with!'

Chris pressed his hand hard on Rasmus' knee before saying the last bit and Rasmus placed his over it, behind the others' backs, before giving him a violent cuff.

'Do you have to get fresh on top of everything, you shit!'

'Hold your tongues, boys!' Mick roared. 'We've got better things to do than worry whether you are bosom pals or not!'

Chris felt as if they had been driving all night. Would he ever be able to travel by car in darkness again without thinking of this particular drive?

'I think it's about time for the handkerchief routine,' said Torben at last.

'Okay.' Mick took something out of a bag and gave it to Rasmus. 'Could you manage to blindfold Christopher? I'll see to you afterwards; I don't want to risk letting go of Henrik more than necessary.'

Rasmus said gleefully that nothing could be easier and began fumbling with the cloth; Chris gave him a slight cuff for safety's sake, but of course it wasn't necessary. Rasmus made a great show of folding the cloth and talking about how thick it was and Chris noticed that he was searching for something in his pocket.

'Don't make any trouble, will you, Christopher?' said Torben.

Chris shrugged his shoulders in the dark. 'What good would that do?' he said irritably.

'It wouldn't, would it?' Rasmus was by no means as bad an actor as he thought he was. He sounded thoroughly

129

nasty, and when the blindfold was in place and Chris put one hand up to it, there was the neatest little tear, right over one eye!

He took the opportunity, while Mick was blindfolding Rasmus, to fumble at it. He must know exactly where it was, so that he could give the blindfold a tweak and be able to see a little at the right moment.

Pierre asked: 'What makes the boy?' and Torben looked in the driving mirror. 'Leave the blindfold alone, lad!'

'I don't want the arm of my specs sticking in my ear!' Chris said irritably, and went on fumbling at the side of his head a moment longer.

Oof! Pierre must have eyes in the back of his head. But they had been fooled, and at the same time he had prepared an excuse for himself to fidget – they would think it was the arm of the glasses again.

'Hey, not this damn way!' Mick burst out.

Torben spoke through clenched teeth. 'We'll go my way as long as I'm at the wheel! The more little tracks and unmade-up roads we use, the better. As you yourself said, they're not all weak in the head, are they? We'd never get in on the usual approach roads without being stopped, once they have the alarm out, and they'll have done that long ago: it's half-past eleven now.'

'Oh, well . . . you sound nervous. Are you?'

'What do you think? I'm not weak in the head either, am I? How long was it he said we were in for, if we were caught? And with Henrik instead of a helping hand, the risk is all the greater, besides the fact that we have never even met this Domenico.'

'We'll be absolutely safe there, at all events.'

Pierre broke in at this point and asked what they were talking about; Torben had sounded quite excited.

130

'We're arguing which road to take; we have to avoid the main approach roads, you see.'

Chris wondered whether Rasmus knew enough English to realize that this was a rather inaccurate translation!

At long last the car began to slow down. 'It's number twenty-eight,' said Torben. 'Would you keep a look out, Mick?'

Number twenty-eight where? Chris was just able to make out a suburban road. Not one he knew. It might be anywhere, in any of the outer suburbs. But at least he knew the number.

Not that it was much use to them, but you never knew. He took another peep while Pierre, who was leading him, stopped to whisper something to Mick, who was following with Henrik.

An open garage door – a car.

He dropped his hand quickly from the blindfold.

9

They were led down some stairs as soon as they were indoors. Through a door to the right at the foot of the stairs . . . 'You can take your blindfolds off now,' said Torben's voice. It sounded tired, and he looked worn and anxious when Chris and Rasmus could see him again, but he pulled himself together and smiled faintly. 'I've got no time now,' he said, 'but we'll bring you something or other soon. At least it's warm here.'

Chris and Rasmus looked at each other when he had gone, locking the door behind him.

'God knows where the devil we are now,' said Rasmus gloomily. Chris said something about there being no point in knowing and laid a warning hand over Rasmus' mouth at the same time. He looked round: two beds, their sleeping-bags thrown onto one of them, a table with some drawers in it, two garden chairs and a naked electric light bulb hanging from the ceiling.

If they used the sleeping-bags . . .

Chris unrolled his silently and Rasmus followed his example, his face one big question-mark. If they put them one on top of the other and talked with their heads underneath, it should be safe.

'First we've got to find out if there are any microphones here,' Chris explained softly, under the sleeping-bags. 'This is an ordinary road; I don't know it, it might be anywhere. But there's a car with CD plates in the garage. It must be a private house, because an Embassy has a plate outside, but you never know.'

'Do you really think someone would put microphones in a cellar?' Rasmus whispered back.

'I don't know, I just think we ought not to talk about private plans when we can't be sure.'

'Okay.'

They crawled out from under the sleeping-bags. 'It's not very cosy here,' said Rasmus aloud.

Chris shrugged his shoulders. 'No, but at least we don't have to look at hypodermics and pot and all that muck. And we don't have to be with them all the time.'

How did you look for microphones? They began with the beds, feeling all over the mattresses and picking them up to look underneath, trying to see if there was anything loose on the bedposts, silently moving the whole bed a little way out and examining the floor. The heater, the light-switch, the table. Chris gently pulled out the drawers. All four were empty. Except . . .

Just before he pushed the last one in again, he saw something white at one side. A scrap of newspaper, caught on a forgotten drawing-pin.

It was tiresome to have to put your heads under the sleeping-bags every time you wanted to discuss something. 'I think it's some kind of Spanish,' Chris whispered. 'Don't you?'

'Haven't the faintest,' said Rasmus glumly. 'It might be.'

'And they were talking about someone called Domenico, in the car. I think that sounds a bit Spanish, too. In South America they kidnap people all the time.'

'Shut up, you idiot! Do you think my father would go along with anything like that?'

'He hasn't gone along with it, has he? He's not in it any more.'

Rasmus took his head out and Chris followed, just in time. They heard footsteps on the stairs and a moment later the door opened. It was Torben, with a large cardboard box. He went out again and brought another in from the stairs.

'Orange juice, transistor, oranges . . . a bit of everything, gentlemen! I shall see if I can get you a TV set for tomorrow, and something to read, and here is the bathroom!'

He put a blue bucket in the corner, beside the basin. Chris looked at it with distaste and Rasmus burst out that that was a bit too damned much.

'Shut up, Ras! All hell has broken loose and I'm so damn' tired . . .'

'You could at least let *me* go to the lavatory properly, it's not me who's been kidnapped, is it?' Rasmus looked challengingly at him.

Torben pushed the hair back from his forehead. '*No*, I said . . . that is, I mean, of course you haven't been kidnapped, but we can't do it any other way, not tonight anyway. Either Viggo or Mick will be sleeping down here with Henrik, but they're not certain to hear you if you knock, and there aren't enough of us in the house to keep watch everywhere; I certainly wouldn't dare to leave you alone with Henrik, in the state he's in, with only one of the others to help. So we are splitting up.'

Rasmus asked where all the others had gone.

'There's not room for us all here. Some of us have something else to look after, too. It was a bloody nuisance that we had to move.'

'It will be all right,' said Chris. 'It's no use making a fuss, Rasmus, and Torben can't do any better than he is doing. Actually I'm reasonably sure that he's the only one who would even have thought we might get thirsty – or the opposite. But you really should be thinking about that safe conduct, Torben!'

Torben put his hand on the door knob. 'I can think till I'm blue in the face . . . The group won't be able to take a decision before tomorrow afternoon! In any case, who says I feel any necessity to think?'

But he did, thought Chris when Torben had gone. And he had not been honest with Pierre in the car. Of course, that might be because he did not want Pierre to know he was nervous. But it *might* also be because he had begun to have second thoughts about the whole affair and was not too keen about Pierre.

'I don't *think* there are any microphones here,' said Chris in a low voice. 'If there are, they must be built into the wall or something. If we almost whisper, when it's something important, I think we can risk talking.'

Rasmus said despondently that it was no good talking either. 'There's just one door here, and not so much as

134

one window – I can't bloody well see how we can get out of this muck-heap anyhow! Not if I can't persuade Torben, and even if I could get permission to go to the lavatory, what then? There's no guarantee that I would be able to get away, even so.'

Chris rummaged in the cardboard box. They might as well share a tin of juice. There were ginger-biscuits, too. So extraordinarily normal – a carton with a familiar label on it and cellophane, as if the outside world were still in existence. He had almost stopped believing in it.

'Can you imagine what your father and mother might be doing?' he asked cautiously. 'I mean, don't you think your father will be looking for you? Perhaps *he* could find his way to us. After all, he knows them – knows who they are, I mean . . .'

Rasmus put the tin of orange down with a thump: 'As if I hadn't been thinking of that for the last two days! You self-satisfied idiot, you think it's only you and your family who . . . Perhaps you imagine my father doesn't care about me?'

'You're talking too loud,' said Chris mechanically.

Rasmus lowered his voice: 'He does, so there! But how the devil can he find them? They're damn' sure to keep away from the places they usually go to; they know they can be sure as shit that he's after them!'

'But Rasmus – oh, do stop flying off the handle, can't you? If your father were to go to the police, or if he could just get hold of Father, quite privately, and tell *him*? With all the information he could give, the police would have a far better chance. My father would certainly understand that it has all turned out quite differently from what your father intended. I heard it myself, so I could be a witness.'

'Perhaps Dad is a bit afraid of *how* different it may be.' Rasmus was talking very quietly and his face was ashen.

Italy and all those other places. Neither of them had referred to it, but it might have been written on the bare cellar wall in large letters. Cripes, what a blithering idiot I am, not to have held my tongue, Chris thought unhappily. Rasmus would never have thought of it for himself, but once you've got him started he's quick enough – and what good does it do for us both to be afraid?

'We mustn't let our imaginations run away with us,' he said, trying to sound encouraging. 'After all, we don't really know anything, it may be just because it's late at night. Your head starts going round and round too easily when you're sleepy. I think we ought to go to bed; we're sure to get an idea tomorrow and it'll all look quite different.'

He didn't believe it himself.

Rasmus fell asleep almost at once, he was so tired; Chris lay awake in the darkness. He noticed that he was sweating with tiredness himself, but how could you sleep when your thoughts were churning round and round?

In the morning there would simply be the same cellar room without windows. And fear.

If only Mick had not called the police 'swine'. Up to that moment it had been possible not to be scared – almost. But once you got frightened you kept thinking of all kinds of things . . . Things that were written in the letters sent to the newspapers when someone was kidnapped. In those countries where they finished up by murdering the hostages if they did not get their way.

Torben wouldn't agree to that!

No, but perhaps he hadn't the power to decide. Perhaps it was too late for him to do anything. Sometimes hostages were killed just because the criminals got frightened when they were close to being discovered. Mr Møller knows that. Father knows too, but he doesn't know that there might be the same kind of people here in Denmark.

Does Mr Møller know that? If so, he wouldn't dare to go to the police.

His head felt as if it were stuffed with clammy cotton-wool. I must think about something else, thought Chris desperately. If I don't think about something else I shall soon be so frightened that I shall get up and start hammering on the door.

It might be pure coincidence: sometimes the activists had foreign students visiting them because they were useful for demonstrations, making partisan stickers and so on. Perhaps there were going to be some more riots soon and that was why Pierre had come. And he was simply lending a hand now because he was here. The one called Domenico, the one who lived here – if he was a diplomat from a country which hadn't got a democracy, he might simply be an ordinary Leftist. Yes, perhaps he didn't even know they were there!

So if they made enough row in the morning until he heard them, he could ring for the police. And Henrik could go to hospital.

If he hung on to that thought, and then thought very hard about a particular chess game he could remember, he might be able to fall asleep.

But he did not sleep well, he kept on waking up and sweating. In the end he decided to turn on the light. Rasmus was sleeping like a stone, his head buried in the sleeping-bag.

Chris crept out and hunted through the cardboard box. He thought he remembered – yes, there it was!

Torben had brought a silly little reading-lamp down here. If he put it on the floor beside the bed and turned off the ceiling light Rasmus would certainly not wake up, because it was only six o'clock. Chris could eat a ginger

137

biscuit and drink some orange juice. Time was so endless, just lying awake in the dark.

Nothing was any better after the little bit of sleep he had had. However much you twisted and turned, you could not get away from the logic of it; it had begun as something stupid and irritating, because it was pointless and tiresome. Mr Møller, who simply had to make a drama out of a perfectly normal referendum. Oh well, perhaps referendums were not all that normal, but at least they were legal. There had been no need to let himself be talked into kidnapping other people's children. It would have been very pleasant at the Møllers, if only he had been there of his own free will; Mrs Møller's marvellous home-made bread and the funny, pretty little sister, and ordinarily, when he was not so busy hating Father, Mr Møller would be kind too. Rasmus was not exactly his number one person, but he had his points and it was probably good to talk to someone you had to take trouble to like.

But from the moment that female arrived with Torben and picked them up, everything started to get worse. The attic at Marieholm, the air of lunacy, with people who just sat and sat and talked and talked, until it felt as if the hours had all run together and time was standing still.

Carl, who noticed nothing but his own voice. Mick and Viggo, who knew what the whole world should be like, when it was their turn to decide. In a way they were even worse than Henning, thought Chris suddenly. You could understand something about Henning. He was evil and almost certainly a mental case, but you could hear when he was frightened and when he wanted something and when he hated people. With Mick and Viggo there was – well, there really was nothing you could get hold of; they even talked in quite a friendly way, when they spoke to one at all.

But it was as if they were already not living in the real world, outside – as if they were already in the one they wanted to build. And there, there was no place for other kinds of people. Perhaps they simply didn't take in that other kinds were real?

Like looking after Henrik, for instance. They did what was necessary, but they neither smiled at him nor were angry with him, nor friendly. None of them seemed to have any use for friendliness.

I don't understand it. How can you get on without it? If you have made a fool of yourself, or your throat hurts, or if you have taken trouble over something; you can't go on without people ever being friendly, or without being friendly yourself.

Torben seems to have changed since I first saw him. Almost as if *he* had begun to feel a need for friendliness. By now he's almost being nice to me. But perhaps it's too late. At Marieholm there were windows, you could see that the world was there, outside, and you knew where you were. Now it's got worse again. We no longer know where we are, we don't know whose house we're in, who's going to decide ... We don't know what's going to happen.

Perhaps we shall be killed, down here, in a windowless cellar, because they'll get frightened of going to prison ... And because they can't use me for anything, anyway.

Rubbish! Chris told himself resolutely. Of course they could kill us, but what on earth would they do with us afterwards? If they don't think of that for themselves, we'll say it. Then they'll have to think again.

But when Rasmus wakes up I must tell him everything I know, about Marieholm and about the chessman. We must write a short message, so that we have it ready if a chance comes up, perhaps if Henrik gets so ill that they

139

can't avoid taking him to hospital. If we could put the paper in his pocket, or something like that . . .

Chris suddenly discovered that he had been gazing up for a long time at an end of pipe in the ceiling, without seeing it. Where could that lead? Perhaps to a radiator which was not in use?

The ceiling was not very high. If he stood on the bed he could reach it. The end of the pipe was filled with a wooden stopper.

'Rasmus! Wake up!' whispered Chris, shaking him gently.

Rasmus' eyes flew open – right open, wide awake on the spot! He really was an extraordinary boy. 'Rasmus, I've seen a bunged-up pipe. If we could get the bung out, so that it can be put back without anyone seeing – a safety-pin or something . . .'

They emptied their pockets, and their brains as well; it was Rasmus who caught sight of the staples in one of the cardboard boxes.

'This is a shi – a brilliant knife,' he said, impressed, when Chris handed it over; his own was not up to much. He levered out the staple and filed one end of it sharp.

'You'd better try,' said Chris, when it was ready. 'You're better with your hands than I am.'

It was weird, seeing such patience in a chap who was otherwise so excitable; as if his fingers belonged to someone else.

'It's coming,' Rasmus whispered at last.

As the stopper came out on the end of the staple, they heard the humming noise of a machine. Chris thought his heart had stopped beating, he was so startled.

Rasmus listened. 'Vacuum cleaner,' he whispered, very softly.

There was nothing to be seen, no light or anything. 'Perhaps there is a carpet over it,' Chris whispered back.

140

Now it would be good to know if anyone ever used that room? But at least it was tremendously encouraging, simply that they had done something, discovered something. Chris peeled a white, self-adhesive price label off an orange and Rasmus rearranged their hook so that it was fixed like a loop. With the white label over it, it was quite invisible, and to get it out or put it back again took only a moment.

Chris put it in; no one would come in during the vacuum cleaning, and they had a lot to talk about.

Rasmus obviously could not make up his mind whether to be impressed or indignant over all that Chris had discovered. Especially the idea of the chessmen. 'Your big brother must be quick on the uptake,' he said reluctantly, 'thinking of putting one in his pocket and showing it too quickly for anyone else to notice. Come to think of it, you're pretty quick on the uptake yourself – getting hold of the marble and taking the chessman right under Carl's nose without him finding out.'

'Yes, but you are much cleverer with your fingers than I am,' said Chris, 'and you've got such incredible patience!'

A big, beaming, delighted grin broke out on Rasmus' face. 'This is something new, isn't it? As soon as you need me, the pipe plays a different tune – you crafty toad!'

Chris found himself grinning too. 'Blithering idiot!' he said. Mostly because it was wonderful to want to smile, just for a moment; and because Rasmus got much nicer and generally good to look at when he smiled. Then he went on, seriously again: 'Rasmus, we all need somebody, can't you see that? Even people who don't particularly like each other, or who disagree completely. I think what's dangerous is when you think other people are so wrong that you sort of shut them out. Because the next

141

thing is that you believe you're entitled to decide that they have no right to exist. Can't you see that?'

Rasmus had put his ordinary expression on again already, except that his eyes were sad instead of angry. 'I don't know,' he said shortly. 'I don't know anything any more – I just wish . . .'

Chris never found out what he wished; someone was coming down the stairs.

Torben. He looked as if he had not been to bed at all. 'Hello,' he said. 'Here's some milk and sandwiches. You can't have anything hot, you'll have to make do with this. Henrik's sleeping or whatever it is he's doing, and Mick is here too, and I have investigated the lavatory. We can take you there one at a time, if it's now . . .'

If only it had been a little later, thought Chris; it's not light yet and I needed to see if any daylight got down here. It's too much to hope that there will be a window in the lavatory. But there was.

The room was not very big and neither was the window, but you could probably just squeeze through it. You could reach it if you stood on the seat, but you couldn't open it, the glass would have to be broken. That didn't give much chance, because the person standing guard outside would hear the row and run round to the window. Even if you were lucky and the brute went the wrong way round, you would be in the worst possible position for a getaway, having just got onto your feet outside.

Apart from the fact that you couldn't count on there being any more lavatory visits during the day . . .

But it was worth knowing: the lavatory was down here, it had a window, and there was a latch with which you could lock the door from the inside. Before he left he picked up an old nail which was lying in the corner, and a bit of wire.

There was no key in the door at the top of the stairs.

On a nail on the wall of the cellar passage hung a shabby overcoat, and in a corner further away there was a worn broom – that was all, except of course for the doors, their own, one beside it and one opposite.

'How do you do it?' asked Rasmus when Chris described the room to him. 'I only saw two doors – oh yes, and the coat out there.'

Rasmus, on the other hand, had remembered to ask Torben for a writing-pad to draw on. At first he had been stubborn and said that Chris was a much better actor, but Chris had been firm.

'You don't have to play-act; we can make the time pass if I try to help you over some of your weak points in maths. The fact that we're going to use the paper for something else doesn't come into it! But *you* must be the one to ask. Perhaps you don't understand this, but I'm not asking those men for anything – I say thank you and take the food – I'm not going to die of hunger; but I have never done anything to them, neither have my family, they don't know me, and yet they still come barging in with their lies and lock me up and order me about and *interfere* in my life – I'm not asking them for anything. I'm not going to owe them so much as a safety-pin!'

Rasmus had agreed quite calmly, but he had stared a bit. A little later he said slyly: 'Zombie?'

'Even zombies can get to a point when they have had enough!'

Perhaps that had been a silly moment to get angry suddenly, but the more tired and worried Torben looked, the more difficult it was to remember that he was the enemy, just like the others. Him and his orange juice! But he had been in on it from the very beginning, it was he who had been the first prison guard and he who had kidnapped Rasmus as well. It was all very well to begin to feel some sympathy for him, just because he had not

143

realized from the beginning that professional terrorists from abroad would be mixed up in this . . .

But now they had the paper, and an extra ball-point pen, because Rasmus naturally hadn't got one. And Torben had come down with a morning paper and a smart little portable television and the news that they would be getting breakfast some time or other.

When his steps faded up the stairs Rasmus removed the stopper in the ceiling and Chris put the paper on the table in order to turn the pages silently.

For some time there was not a sound from the hole in the ceiling; the newspaper, on the other hand, was practically full of the case.

'Do stop reading so fast,' whispered Rasmus crossly. 'You turn over before I'm half-way down the page.'

But you didn't need to read it all, line by line; Chris had learned that from Father. Father had to read so many papers and he did not have much time to spare. He had shown Chris how to see quickly what the real news was and what was mere padding; for instance, people were asked to make statements, and with a photograph of them as well, they made excellent padding.

But you didn't need to read through it all to see that everyone was furious about the kidnapping – not one single person had dared to defend it publicly, not even that journalist who always sounded as if he were bursting with hatred for everything. Well, of course he said that it was Father who had provoked the action, but he did not dare to say right out in the newspaper that it was a good idea.

There were more photographs: the one Mother had taken on the terrace and, good heavens, a feeble old school photograph from the year before. Fortunately he wasn't the only one in it who looked like an idiot.

The only real news was that the police had received a

tip yesterday – 'an anonymous message', it said, which had led them to investigate 'a castle in south Zealand'. The investigation 'produced no results, but there were several clues to be followed up'.

And then it said that they had been in touch with the owner, who was abroad, and it had been proved that he hadn't had anything at all to do with the kidnapping, he had simply lent a studio to the well-known painter Henning Jansen for the winter months.

Chris could have shouted with relief; not that it changed anything, it did not bring him any nearer home and it was not as if he knew the old Baron very well, either. But it had been so frightening to think that such a wise, kind old gentleman could be a traitor – as if there were no longer any order in anything. Sometimes, in the night, that thought had made it seem as if the whole world he knew had simply ceased to exist, that it was the female's and the others' hate world which was the real one, and that he himself had simply been living inside an invisible little box, with the remnants of some other old-fashioned objects which no longer existed outside.

It had been so – so *evil*, to think that the only kind of world you knew and could cope with, simply didn't exist. Thank goodness it was not true. Wise old Baron Corfeldt was exactly what Chris had believed him to be. How on earth had Henning managed to fool him into inviting him there?

10

'Ssshh!'

Chris looked up in surprise; he hadn't said a word.

Yes, a door had opened upstairs! They both sat down on Chris's bed and concentrated on listening.

'Now, damn it, I want to have some idea what's going on!' It was Torben's voice. 'I like it less and less. It's obvious now that we can't get anywhere with our demands, and I'm not keen about Henrik's condition either. If he goes and dies on our hands, what then? What is the position, if you don't call in help and someone dies?'

A voice which was too far away to be heard clearly said something and Torben replied that this was no time for fine phrases: of course he didn't recognize the corrupt legal machinery of the system, either, but that was certainly not going to stop it from operating.

So it was Carl who had spoken.

There was Carl's voice: he said that Henrik's life was beyond saving anyway; and then came a long stream of his usual, long-winded, phony speech-making about the revolution and the working people and profiteers; the situation was grave and they would have to take the wide view and the point had now been reached at which if you wanted to make omelettes you had to break eggs.

Chris's fists had clenched before he knew it. It was Henrik who was to be broken – Henrik who had been

146

pleasant and gentle – Henrik, who believed that happiness was making yourself part of other people – Henrik, the only one who was prepared to wash up or do anything at all which was a nuisance. It was Henrik who could be allowed to die, just to save the others' skins!

Perhaps he would die anyway, perhaps he could never be well enough for something to be made of his life. But it was not *Carl*'s right to decide that Henrik should go to waste.

'Where is Mick, and when is this Wilfred coming?' asked Torben.

A woman's voice answered, a pleasantly soft, gentle woman's voice which Chris did not think he knew: 'Mick is at a meeting. We have to distract people's attention from the boy. It's very tricky getting a disturbance organized at a moment's notice, without having time to create some provocation, but feeling will run against us if we can't get that boy off the front pages. We've tried to find something disreputable about him which might cool the indignation down a bit, but we've had no luck, unfortunately. He's such a conformist and so ordinary that his teachers *and* his friends have nothing but praise for him.'

'Why the hell don't we send the boys home, Yutta?' said Torben. So it was the 'female' who had such a pretty voice! 'I've seen more of Christopher than you have; to judge by Christopher himself, I wouldn't be surprised if Egstrup kept his word, if he came home before the safe conduct runs out. And no one knows anything about Rasmus. Mogens is sure to hold his tongue. Why the devil did you people have to change the conditions? We might have managed to get a referendum.'

Then they all began to talk at once about what else they might have done and what they might try to achieve now by standing firm.

'You know quite well that we can't decide until Wilfred comes,' Yutta said.

'—Says who!' You could hear Torben was angry now. '—Who *is* this mysterious Wilfred whom none of our group has met? And whose is this house, and the car with its diplomatic number plates? You people come barging into our group with your offers of help . . . all right, you are Carl's friends . . . we're not so bloody dumb that we don't know you have other connections . . . but it was strictly agreed that this was our show . . . your part was to help, *not* to take over, and plunge us into a bloody mess we didn't ask about and don't want to know anything about. I like the whole thing less and less, and you can bloody well tell your precious Wilfred that! And tell him to get us away from this foreigner's hospitality, before everything gets completely out of hand!'

And then there was a crash, as if a chair had been overturned.

'Could we just discuss *my* abused hospitality for a moment!' shouted Henning. 'The rest of you can look after yourselves, but what about me? There I sat, cosy as the yolk in an egg – lovely place, cellars which the senile old fool can't keep count of – I give you house-room, out of sympathy for a common cause, and what thanks do I get! Goodbye to completely free lodgings, the police on my tail . . .'

He sounded shrill with fear and nervousness, completely hysterical. Well, that wasn't so strange. After all, he was a coward to begin with. And perhaps he hadn't even known beforehand that they were going to descend on him down at Marieholm, with hostages and everything! It would be just like Yutta to move in without as much as a "Please"!

Torben said angrily that he could thank Ellen for that. 'The time *I* took buying stuff for those blasted kids, four items here, four items there, so as not to arouse suspicion, but Ellen, that dumb broad, just trots into the nearest supermarket and buys tinned food for the whole company, day in, day out!'

Henning spoke again. Now his voice was suddenly a full octave lower, and threatening: 'Our friend here would do well to have a look in his desk drawer! It might not be too difficult to organize an extra passport, and I'm sure you'll make me a present of an air ticket when you have thought it over. I could just do with a nice long holiday in a pleasant climate – it might even earn a little forgetfulness on my part . . .'

'You are and always will be a deceitful rat, Henning.' Imagine being in agreement with the female, for once!

'Yutta . . .' This was Torben again, speaking impatiently: 'Why don't we now state the condition we first agreed on? Mogens' demand for a referendum? That would at least be *something.*'

'You don't imagine that would do anything but give a thundering majority to the bleeding conformists?'

Yes, now you could certainly tell that it was the female – that contempt for ordinary people. Then of course Carl had to start droning on about the majority being misled and manipulated and therefore not fit to be involved in things which needed a firm hand if one were to achieve a just society . . .

Chris could not help looking at Rasmus. Then he wished he had not. Two enormous tears were rolling down his cheeks – he had not even noticed them himself. It must be ghastly to sit there, hearing that someone had turned your own father into a traitor. But Mr Møller could not be blamed for all this; after all, this was not what he had intended.

Chris would have liked to hear Torben's answer, but someone else came in at that point. It must be Domenico, the person who lived in this house; at all events he spoke English with an extraordinary accent.

And how he grumbled! He obviously knew both Pierre and Wilfred but he had quite obviously not realized that the whole gang would be meeting here in the evening. He talked on and on about 'the cause' and especially about how 'it was his task to promote any liberation movement, anywhere' and 'how could he do it, when they put his security and diplomatic status at risk' by stuffing his cellar full of kidnapped Prime Minister's sons.

'You must go,' he said. 'I can't have the house full of people who don't usually come here. Put the patient in with the boys, then Pierre can see to the guard duty on his own. One of you can come back in the afternoon with food for them, and perhaps I shall have heard from Wilfred by then – if he's coming at all!'

Yutta said that she could not imagine Wilfred letting them down now, when everything depended on the reports he brought with him.

'Can't you?' said Domenico. 'It's time you realized that revolutions are not brought about by wishful thinking! The police may not be particularly bright, but they are not as easily fooled as you tried to make us believe. You can't get near the airport for police and it's the same at all the frontiers. There's not a boy between ten and fifteen who gets on board a boat without being put through a special check. Wilfred's papers are good, but I'm not sure if they're good enough to get him here under those conditions!'

It sounded as if some of them at least were getting ready to go, and Chris replaced the stopper hastily.

'We'd better get that note written now!' he said softly. 'It has to be ready before they come in with Henrik. After that we can't be sure we'll get the chance.'

Rasmus nodded but went on sitting where he was.

I must do it myself, thought Chris. If only I knew if I dared write it all down? If they find the note and discover how much we know, they will never let us go. And Rasmus is completely innocent. Perhaps they won't anyway – the activists would not be in favour, but the others they have drawn in are much more used to shooting off in all directions. That Domenico, not to speak of that Wilfred, who must be a terrorist anyway, since he's travelling with false papers.

Chris sat down at the table and wrote, as small as he could:

South American diplomat's house, number 28. Domenico. French student Pierre. Drug addicts. Danger!

Christopher Egstrup

It looked ridiculously childish, writing 'Danger' like that, but he had to call attention to it, so they would have to think him a baby and a funk, and hurry up for that reason.

Because it *was* dangerous, deadly dangerous. The newspapers and all the ordinary, normal Danes naturally still thought that this was simply a bunch of crazy activists and the usual rioting students. They could not know that they had been joined by real terrorists from abroad.

And I don't think Torben and Mick can stop it now, thought Chris. They are the only ones who probably want to, now they realize what's happening. The female and Carl and Viggo are beyond saving; they are so far out in the world they haven't even created yet that they simply could not stand being ordinary, normal human beings with no more rights than anyone else. Henning only goes along with it because he thinks it's exciting, apart from the fact that he's so afraid for his own skin that I think he would shoot us down just to get away from the police – if he had anything to shoot with, that is.

Chris folded the paper into a tiny square; then he took one of little Tina's marbles and attached the square to it with another sticky label from the oranges.

'Rasmus!' he said softly. 'Don't get upset. Your father would rather have let himself be cut in half than go along with the others if he had realized what was going on – you know that yourself! Even Torben feels now that it's gone too far – getting these foreign terrorist people mixed up in it, I mean, and letting them decide how Danes should arrange things in Denmark. But you must pull yourself together now, Rasmus, do you hear? Domenico is sending all the Danes away. They are going to put Henrik in here with us and set Pierre on guard. So we shall be quite alone in the house with one man who is crazy and can't even stand on his own feet, and two foreigners. We have only ourselves to rely on; we can argue afterwards about what the world ought to be like, but *for God's sake*, let's stand together now and help each other so that there *is* an "afterwards"!'

'Oh, hold your tongue, man, how you go on! I'm not deaf, am I?'

'Sorry,' said Chris automatically. 'Rasmus, I've written everything down, what we know about the address here and Pierre, and stuck it onto one of Tina's marbles; if only Henrik gets ill enough so that in the end they don't dare do anything but take him to hospital, we can get it into his pocket. You can get Pierre to look at something or other on the television for just a moment. But I must be sure that you agree about us doing this, because if they find the paper it's more dangerous than . . . I mean, they would be able to work out that we know too much. But we *must* try to get help, mustn't we?'

'Hold your tongue, can't you? If you could stop just for a moment being so wonderful that it makes me sick! There's a risk if they discover how much we know. Okay!

You're here because of *your* father. But I'm also here because of *my* father. There's no shitting reason why you should take extra care because of me. I understand all about it, and the note is okay by me. Give me your penknife a moment.'

Chris handed it over. 'What do you want to do with it?'

'Just look at it, hold it in my hand, see what it can do . . .'

Chris turned cold all over. 'Rasmus! You're not thinking of doing something on your own?'

'You think I'm a complete idiot, don't you?'

'No, but you're a hothead. You rush in first and think afterwards, when it's too late. We won't have a chance unless we work so closely together that each of us almost guesses what the other is thinking.'

'How the blazes can we?' said Rasmus hotly. 'I never damn' well know what you're thinking, except that it's damn' well the opposite. Here's your knife.'

Chris had already put out his hand for it, but then he changed his mind. 'It's better for you to have it,' he said, trying to make his voice sound quite normal. 'You're better with your hands.'

Rasmus gazed at him in astonishment. 'You're off your head, man! You rely on me, when you simply can't stand me.'

'Put it in your pocket before they come. And I can stand you, actually, sometimes. But even if I couldn't, you *can* rely on people who irritate you; don't be so one-track, you idiot! You get everything mixed up, ideas and people and everything. Two people can disagree till the cows come home and still both be decent. But promise that you won't start anything on your own?'

Rasmus put the knife in his pocket. 'Why should you decide everything?' he said sullenly.

'Because I'm the one who's the zombie,' said Chris pleasantly.

'And what if they just *leave* Henrik here, and that Frenchman? We can't do anything with Henrik in here. You saw for yourself that he runs completely amok if the slightest thing happens anywhere near him. So how are we to get the message out? And if we can't, how are we ever to get out ourselves?'

Rasmus' voice shook a little, and Chris pulled himself together sharply; if they admitted to each other how frightened they were, they would end up being unable to think at all. 'I don't know,' he said, yawning. 'Let's take one thing at a time, shall we? And think about it – it's Pierre who's going to be in here, and he doesn't understand Danish. If you . . . we . . . take care to sound as if we were talking about quite unimportant things, we can say what we like. Perhaps there will be a chance . . .'

He didn't believe it himself. Once Pierre was in here, they could not even use their listening hole.

I'm afraid, he thought. I'm afraid of their hate; it's as if they just *look* like human beings outside. Inside, all the normal, human part has been scraped out and they've been stuffed with hate. There was no possibility of talking to hate, in a way it was like poison gas, there was no solution but to run hell for leather, and hope that you were running fast enough.

And run was just what they could not do. There was no hope at all, apart from Henrik.

And nothing was going to come of that hope, either, thought Chris half an hour later. Pierre had put Henrik in the room, but he just lay quite still; it was only from the colour of his face that you could see he was very ill. It was not bad enough for them to take the risk of driving

154

him to hospital, and there was no other possibility of getting the marble and the note out of the house.

Pierre brought in an extra chair and sat reading a book, but Chris and Rasmus did not talk to each other very much. They knew that Pierre did not understand Danish, but it was difficult to believe it altogether. Then Rasmus thought they could look at Schools' Television from Sweden. The time dragged on until the next news bulletin.

The period for the safe conduct had expired, they said, and the police had begun to question people who had previously been involved in disturbances following demonstrations.

Pierre looked up from his book and asked if they understood English. Rasmus said: 'Very, very little,' and Chris added: 'Only the teachers, at school'.

Then Pierre tried pointing at the radio and asking what had been said. Both boys shook their heads and Chris said: 'News', and shook his head again. Pierre gave up.

More time dragged past. Chris took an orange and began to peel it, really to make the time pass; then, at last, there was someone on the cellar steps.

Imagine actually being glad to see Torben!

'Hello, boys – I'm afraid it's sausages again.'

They had no chance to answer, because Pierre at once began to talk to Torben, trying to find out if there was any news. Torben answered impatiently that he knew nothing, he had enough to do feeding the kids and getting demonstrations going. 'We must keep the police busy, they are beginning to get fresh, the stupid swine, running about asking everyone they can think of.'

Suddenly there was a scream from Henrik and they all turned in time to see him pointing at Chris and rising shakily to his feet. 'The sun! Torben, help! That's why the earth is being destroyed: Christopher has got hold of the sun. Ah, God, he's torn it to bits!'

155

It was only at the last moment that Torben caught him, and Pierre had to help hold him off, as he went on yelling that the sun was being destroyed and Chris must die. Torben hung on with one hand, with the other trying a little awkwardly to smooth a strand of hair back from Henrik's wet brow. 'There now, Henrik,' he said, his voice quite gentle – 'Christopher wouldn't do a thing like that . . . you know that . . . steady now, Henrik . . .'

Chris looked at Rasmus, standing by the wall, staring appalled at the three young men on the floor. Quickly he grabbed a whole orange, pulling the little marble out of his pocket at the same time. 'Henrik, look, Henrik! You were wrong, it hasn't been destroyed at all.' It was difficult to make his voice heard as Henrik struggled to free himself. 'Henrik, look here, there's nothing the matter with the sun. Come on, I'll put it in your own pocket and you can look after it.'

He seemed to become a little quieter, as if he were at least trying to listen. Then, quick as a flash, Torben knocked him out with a punch on the jaw.

Pierre looked down at Henrik, who was lying quite still. 'Better you give he somesing.'

Torben said shortly that he had nothing, and no one would dare to sell pot while the police had their noses into everything. 'I'll take him with me, Pierre. I'll drop him off somewhere where he'll be found and helped; his talk is quite crazy and he has no idea where he is, so there's no risk in letting him be found – and he can't stay here, you can see that yourself, man! You and the boys can't hold him alone, and he just might murder the three of you!'

Pierre asked what Henrik had said and when Torben explained Pierre shrugged his shoulders and agreed. 'But you'll have to do it yourself. I'm staying here.'

The key was turned in the lock behind them and Chris

156

and Rasmus looked at each other and sat down on their own beds. Just in time. Chris had a feeling that if his bed had not been here he would have sat down on the floor with a thud.

'Well, I'm damn well not interested in hash any more,' said Rasmus at last, his voice shaking.

Chris stretched himself out full length and closed his eyes. 'I got the marble into his pocket, under the orange,' he said, his voice faltering. 'I think I'll go to sleep for a bit now.'

11

When he woke up, Pierre was in his chair and Rasmus was glued to the television. He closed his eyes again. What time was it? He had no desire to wake up. Everything was so hopeless when you were awake, like an evil dream.

Perhaps someone would come soon; perhaps Henrik had gone to hospital and someone had found Tina's marble and the message it carried of their whereabouts.

But perhaps they hadn't. Perhaps they had just put everything into a bag without examining it and let it lie in a cupboard. Or perhaps the marble had fallen out on the road and Torben had found it. You could not keep your courage up the whole time, not over such long stretches, not when everything just got worse and worse.

Now there was someone on the cellar steps. Rasmus

looked up, and then across at Chris. Chris winked at him and closed his eyes again.

Ah, so that was what Domenico looked like.

Without even saying good morning, he started talking to Pierre, asking first, in English, how much the boys understood. Pierre said 'Nothing'.

Domenico was afraid that some member of the group would grass when the police questioned them. 'One or two of them were not all that enthusiastic when they heard that Wilfred was coming, but it's the painter I really have no faith in; one can hope that the others will be loyal to the cause even if they are doubtful about directives from outside. But I don't trust the painter, he would do absolutely anything to save his own skin. I know the type.'

As if that were not exactly what he himself was trying to do! thought Chris.

'All in all, I'm not at all happy about the situation. There are too many amateurs mixed up in it; who is to say that they have been careful enough in front of the boys? I understand that the second one was taken along to ensure that his father would not talk – obviously one of those blasted idealists who believe in a heaven on earth. Now listen to me, I've got a party with the Italians at six o'clock; I daren't stay away, a sharp eye is being kept on the whole Diplomatic Corps, except for their own allies. I'll get away as quickly as I can and then we shall have to discuss whom to get rid of. Yutta is all right, and Viggo; Carl doesn't understand anything but his own tirades and he is an excellent "cover", but those two who always stick up for each other – what are they called? Yes, Torben and Mikael – I'm not so sure about them; they seem to me a bit too independent. Heaven preserve us from a gang of dilettanti! And why the hell they kidnapped the boy without knowing precisely how far they could go in their demands . . .'

Chris peeped out through his eyelashes and saw Pierre shrug his shoulders. 'What's done is done. We realize that this country is not ripe – yet.'

'That's very good,' sneered the other, 'but who's going to have to clear up after this fiasco? You and me and Yutta – and it will have to be before the others realize that we can't let the boys go home and describe us all. Well, you can manage for an hour or two. Fernando is keeping watch outside, so there's no one but the cook in the house, but it's better if you stay down here. He's pretty hard of hearing, but all the same . . .'

Pierre asked if the other had any ideas.

'Hypodermics for four,' said Domenico shortly. 'And enough to blow up a car. Yutta will have to get the car.'

Chris had never known that you could faint lying down, but he must have been completely gone for a moment, because he had not heard Domenico leave; yet now there was no one there but Pierre, and Rasmus who was asking what they had said, so impatiently that Chris realized it must be for the second time.

'Hang on a bit. Turn on the television, so that it looks as if we're talking about that.'

Rasmus switched on Swedish Children's Hour, while Chris struggled with a feeling that his head was filled with cottonwool, while before his eyes was a picture of a burned-out car and some charred skeletons.

They had talked about it as if it were a perfectly normal thing to poison four people and then dispose of them so that there were no clues!

How could your opinions make you believe you had the right to turn a live human being into a lump of dead flesh? A strange human being, who had never done anything to you? But it was not going to happen! Or, at all events, they would have to fight to make it happen!

A fight meant that they would shoot, and that would hurt even more, he supposed. But one of us might have a chance, thought Chris. If I think hard, if I don't let myself get frightened, but just sufficiently furious to be able to think.

But would he be able to make Rasmus believe him? After all, he had known most of the Danes before and he was used to hearing about all the things they were going to do and how good and just everything was going to be. One could not expect it to have sunk in, in the course of a few days, that only those who obeyed would have justice, that the people who wanted to decide for themselves could be murdered, by right, as if they were merely . . .

'Tell me what they said, Chris,' said Rasmus softly. He turned his head just for a moment before looking back at the television, but it was enough. His eyes had looked different, as if they had grown darker all of a sudden.

He must have understood a little of what they were saying, thought Chris. He knows there is something wrong.

'Go on watching the television,' he said, sitting up as if he were watching too. 'And make sure you don't give yourself away. I've got a plan, or at least the beginning of one, but it's pretty unpleasant.'

'Don't waffle so much, get to the point, man,' said Rasmus, quite casually, as if he had been talking about Donald Duck.

'That Spaniard said to this one here that they couldn't let us go because the others had let us see and hear too much. They are thinking of killing us, Rasmus, before Torben or any of the others find out about it.'

Rasmus gave a gasp, but fortunately a fire-engine

roared onto the screen at the same moment and Pierre, who had looked up quickly, raised his book again.

'How?'

'We're to have a poisonous injection, which kills us, and then they put us in a car and blow the whole thing up.' Chris tried to make his voice completely casual too. 'Actually it sounded as if they intend to kill T and M as well. They don't trust them, the Spaniard said . . .'

Chris forced himself to give a kind of laugh about Donald Duck, who was swaying to and fro on a ladder, and Rasmus quickly added a 'Ha ha!' of his own.

'We must catch the right moment. If I don't bungle it badly I can get this one down here on the floor, because I know a bit of Judo. Then we'll let ourselves out with his key and break the glass in the lavatory and crawl out that way.'

Rasmus said that it all sounded very simple.

'Yes, but it's not,' said Chris honestly. 'In the first place, don't be fooled by him sitting reading, he's keeping an eye on everything we do. And in the second – cripes, man! don't you realize that he's got a gun in the pocket of his anorak? We run the risk of its going off and hitting us.'

'It won't do that,' said Rasmus, quite calmly. 'He can't be quite such an idiot as to sit about with a gun with the safety-catch off in his pocket. If he does, the . . . the . . . murderer, there's a shitting good chance that he would shoot himself every time he turned the page!'

'I *see*! But Rasmus, it's deadly dangerous all the same, because I could get scared just at the wrong moment and miss; and even if we get this one here out of it, there's still a guard outside in the garden, another foreigner. If he hears us breaking the glass, or if we can't find our way out of a garden we don't know, in the dark – if this one here is armed, the one outside will be too. Don't answer right away, otherwise it won't look as if we were watching the TV.'

After a silence, Rasmus said thoughtfully: 'That bit about darkness works both ways. I can hear that it's raining and there can't be a moon right now, so if we don't land up on an open garden path, he can only hit one of us, at best, and probably only in the leg or something like that . . .'

Chris thought to himself that he had no great desire to be shot in the leg either, but Rasmus' optimism was a help now, at least. 'If we're going to do it, it must be while the Spaniard is out, at that party. But we *could* just leave it, Rasmus – it's possible that Henrik is in hospital by now and that they've found the marble with the information.'

He almost hoped the other would think they should wait and rely on being found. Who could tell if his grip would be sure enough, when he knew it was a matter of life and death? In that case, Pierre would shoot. He wouldn't dare to take any chances . . .

'No, thanks very much! I've no intention of sitting here, meek as a lamb, waiting for them to come and kill me with poison and blow me up afterwards! That shower of foreign murderers!'

'But it was Danes who invited them in,' said Chris seriously, 'and do be careful not to shout! People like Yutta and Viggo. As soon as you begin to hate people instead of ideas, I think it's the most dangerous thing in the world, because it always ends up in people believing they have the right to kill other people who are in their way. This one with us now – he simply doesn't see two boys who have never done a thing to him. We are just two objects which are in the way. And ever since they agreed that we should be killed, he's looked at us as if we were already *dead* objects.'

162

Rasmus did not answer. The Donald Duck film was over now, and he switched to Denmark; there they were in the middle of a film about a boy and a kite, so he went back to the edge of his bed.

'How long before we give it a try?' was all he said.

Chris squinted at his watch. 'Half an hour, more or less.'

'Can you explain to me exactly what you want to do and what I ought to do?'

'I must make him fall hard, on his head, preferably so that he's unconscious for a moment. It's lucky there's a stone floor here. For safety's sake I'll hold his right arm until you have the pistol. But if he doesn't fall hard enough, we'll have to bash his head on the floor until he's unconscious.'

Rasmus said that that would be a pleasure to him.

'I've got some string in my anorak, what about the one you've got in your trousers? I can wriggle mine out while we're watching this film; the anorak is in a position where he can't see it, if I do it a little at a time. We'll have to wait for *yours*, but if it goes according to plan there should be time for that too before he wakes up.'

'And a sock in his mouth,' said Rasmus enthusiastically.

'The most difficult thing will be getting him into the right position,' Chris said. 'I must get close to him, and as much in front of him as possible. Now we'll be quiet again for a bit.'

For one thing it mustn't sound like a continuous conversation, he thought, and for another, Rasmus may get an idea.

The boy in the film was running at full speed across a meadow, to get the kite up. It was a strangely unreal thought – running around free, out in the open, out in the world, just being a schoolboy with a day off, who could

163

go home for lunch. It was difficult to remember having known all that.

'If you say the word, just beforehand,' said Rasmus slowly, without taking his eyes from the screen, 'I'll pretend I have to adjust the set a bit; I know how to make the picture keep rolling up. Then I'll sit down again and when we see it rolling we'll both make signs or something, to get him to see if he can put it right.'

'. . . and if he does it, when we're all three standing up, could you manage to give him a push? Just a little, as if it were only because we were standing too close together, and then get out of the way like lightning to give me room?'

Rasmus said okay.

'I want him to have most of his weight on one foot, you see.'

Rasmus said okay again and they stopped talking.

I don't want to die now, Chris thought. I don't know what death is, I only know the word. I don't know how you go about dying. I want to go home to Father and Mother and Jørgen. I might like to go home with Rasmus once or twice and argue with him and play with his little sister and eat some of Mrs Møller's home-made bread. I want to take the University exam and by that time I would know what I want to be. I want to *have* my life – I don't want to stay down in a cellar with no windows and be just something which has to be got out of the way.

Mrs Møller and Rasmus' little sister. If only he could think of a way to keep Rasmus' father out of this altogether – or almost, at least. Now if Torben and the others had kidnapped him and taken him straight to Marieholm, they might have taken Rasmus later, then his father need not have known anything about their plan.

If only he didn't get so tired of thinking all the time! In the end it felt as if you were walking into the sea, against

164

the waves, walking and walking and scarcely moving from the spot.

If he and Rasmus were to stick to that story – if he could warn his father and mother – then it would be our word against the others. Perhaps even Torben and Mick would be so sorry, when they saw how things were going, that they would not even say it was a lie . . .

If, if, if, thought Chris. If the two of us are not dead in twenty minutes . . . Dear Lord, couldn't You take a hand in this? I know I'm always forgetting the Lord's Prayer before I go to sleep, so perhaps it's pretty low to come running to You just because I need help – but You say that You never judge by whether one is good enough, and I don't think we're going to make it without help from someone besides each other . . . And . . . well, there is only You, isn't there? I don't forget to say Our Father on purpose, it's just because I'm such a nightbird . . . so if You could please help us a little bit . . . Amen.

It seemed to help – perhaps he should have promised to remember to say the Lord's Prayer in future? No, it would have been like a bribe, and that surely wasn't on – trying to bribe God!

'We'll use that overcoat out there for smashing the glass,' he said in a low voice. 'You remember to shoot the bolt, while I knock the pane out and crawl out first . . .'

'Why should you take the biggest risk?'

'I can't see that one risk is any greater than the other – it's the most practical thing to do, because I'm thinner and you're a bit taller, so you can get up there easier on your own. We'll look for cover at once and keep quite still for a bit until we know if the guard has heard anything. Then we'll each crawl off on our own, or, if he has heard us, we'll each run for it. He'd have to be very lucky to hit us both. The other must *run*, do you

165

understand? Straight to the first house with a light on. As soon as one of us gets away, the other is safe.'

'Do you think so?' said Rasmus doubtfully.

'They're not interested in being arrested for wilful murder, you ass! They'll try and talk themselves out of it.'

Unless the guard gets desperate, thought Chris; but there was no point in saying that aloud.

Time passed. Then Rasmus said reluctantly: 'I say, Chris. You're not actually quite as dim as I thought.'

'Idiot!' said Chris pleasantly.

The film must be over soon. Chris stole a look at his watch. The Spaniard must have gone now – better get it over before he was so frightened that he couldn't lift a finger. 'Now,' he said quietly.

Rasmus got up and fiddled with the television. Then he sat down again. It seemed an age to Chris before the picture began to roll – at last!

And suddenly everything was moving incredibly fast. Pierre got up when Rasmus tugged at his sleeve and began unwillingly to fiddle about with the set. The three of them were standing close together now. Chris caught Rasmus' eye and instantaneously, it seemed, Rasmus swayed off balance and pushed Pierre from one side.

There wasn't enough room; afterwards Chris never knew how it had come off. Perhaps it was because he did not want to be forced to bash a man's head against a cement floor. In a flash he had hooked one leg round Pierre's left, which was taking most of his weight, and thrown all his strength into pushing his head back. Crack! it went.

'He went out like a light!' cried Rasmus delightedly.

'Ssshh! Get the string out of your trousers! First get hold of that pistol!'

Chris held on with one hand to Pierre and with the

other grabbed his anorak-string from the bed; Rasmus had already fished the pistol out of Pierre's pocket. 'Let me! I'll tie his hands while you pull my trouser cord out!'

Chris's hands were shaking so much that he could scarcely untie the knot. Then it came and while Rasmus bound Pierre's ankles together as well, Chris pulled off his shoe and one sock.

Rasmus tore it out of his hands. 'Let me, you zombie! There! He'll have to do quite a bit of spitting before he gets that out again,' he said triumphantly.

What Chris most wanted was to be sick, but there was no time for that. The key was in Pierre's left trouser pocket; he got hold of it just as the man's eyes opened.

'Give me the pistol,' said Chris hoarsely.

'What are . . .'

'Give it to me!' hissed Chris. 'You've got my knife!'

'Okay.'

'Let's go – here's the key.'

Chris put the pistol in his pocket; it was best that Rasmus shouldn't have it. He was at white heat, to judge by his expression.

'Take it easy,' said Chris, as evenly as he could. He took the old overcoat off the nail in the passage, and made it look as if they had plenty of time. Inside the lavatory all he said was: 'Bolt the door, Rasmus.'

There was scarcely enough room for the two of them. Chris took a deep breath.

'Now I'll smash the glass as quietly as I can. You be ready to push from behind, to get me up. As soon as I'm out, get up on the lavatory seat and follow me. I'll have a hand ready.'

'You're clearing off!'

'Shut up, Rasmus,' said Chris calmly. 'We can argue later.'

He put the coat against the pane and pushed, pulled

167

away a bit more glass and heard it tearing his clothes as he crawled out. Something dug into one hand – it hurt like blazes. Then he was up and out and turning round just as Rasmus grasped the window-frame with one hand.

'Just shove off! I'm ready to pull.'

He could only use his right hand to pull with, the other felt strangely useless.

'Get the hell out!' whispered Rasmus.

'Have you cut yourself?'

'Zombie! Get away from here!'

It was almost impossible to see anything. Chris ran, crouching, towards a shadow which looked like a bush and saw from the corner of his eye that Rasmus was doing the same. Then both of them stood quite still, one on each side of the bush.

Chris was panting for breath and gripping the hand which hurt. It felt sticky. The light from the road did not reach this far.

Never again would he experience anything so strange as standing, quiet as a mouse, waiting to get close enough to – the enemy.

If only Rasmus would get going! The guard was hesitating; he took a few steps and listened again, said something which sounded like a question; probably something like 'Is there anyone there?'

Yes, there is! thought Chris, suddenly beside himself with rage. That great idiot of a Rasmus was still standing there and jolly well wasn't going to move until Chris did! And I haven't the faintest idea how to get this cocked so that I can fire. I shall just have to jump him, and I shall have to use the wrong hand, because I can't feel the other at all.

All this time, the man was balancing on one foot, which gave Chris his chance to knock him over. Then there was a quiet little 'plop', and a gasp from Rasmus on the other side of the bush, before the man fell.

Chris grabbed hold of something or other – it was Rasmus – and pushed him towards the place from which the guard had come. It was like dragging a sack of cement.

'Clear out, Chris, damn it! He's shot me in the thigh.'

'Shut up, you idiot!' snarled Chris, continuing to drag him. He was at the gate now – now he was right outside – three houses down the street all the lights were on, if only his knees had not been getting more and more weak and woolly . . .

'Chris! Chris, you ZOMBIE! I can limp, if you will just give me a hand.'

But he only had one, and there was a mist in front of his eyes . . .

He had almost collapsed with the strain of getting Rasmus up onto the sound leg; we're not going to make it, he thought. There are three houses before the one with the lights on, and a street light in between, and I didn't use enough force when I pushed him, he may get the pistol loaded again.

Strange – he almost didn't care. It was hard luck on Father and Mother and Jørgen, but if the whole world was different from what he had believed, if there was only that little invisible box he had been living in, and otherwise nothing but hate and violence . . .

He automatically moved close to the fence, where it was darkest.

'Hold that hand in the air,' gasped Rasmus between limps. 'You're bleeding like a stuck pig.'

Now they were past the street lamp. Chris shook his head to clear the mist before his eyes. 'I say, if we make it, Rasmus, I'm going to say that Torben and the others took me straight to Marieholm. I haven't been in your house at all – agreed? Your father didn't know anything about it beforehand, they just took you to threaten him . . .'

Rasmus had scarcely the breath to answer: 'The others . . .' he whispered.

'It's our word against theirs, and I think Torben and Mick will keep quiet.'

There had been no shot.

And he didn't seem to feel quite so weak and woolly when he held his hand up. Chris propped Rasmus up on the garden gate in front of the lighted house and then half staggered, half ran up the garden path, up some steps, fell against a door, put his hand on the bell and held it there while he leaned dizzily against the railing.

A woman came out and screamed.

'Excuse me, I would like to telephone,' he said, as politely as he had breath to speak. 'And Rasmus . . . down by the gate . . .'

The woman gazed at him in horror – then she seemed to take a closer look. 'Are you Christopher Egstrup?' she said. 'My dear boy, what do you look like! Sit here while I get a towel.'

'Telephone,' said Chris again. '. . . and Rasmus . . . get him . . .'

The woman said 'of course,' and called to someone in the other room. 'You can't telephone while you're fainting from loss of blood, Christopher. Svend, go down to the garden gate – there's another one there. Give me a towel first.'

The elderly gentleman looked as if he would have liked to say something, but he went off without a word and the lady held Chris's hand up while he fetched the towel. 'Get Rasmus,' whispered Chris.

'I'm getting him now. Give the boy some cognac, Marianne.'

Ugh, it burned his throat.

'Tell me the number and I'll dial it for you.'

At last . . . Father's voice!

'Father, send the police right away, they've got guns, it's number twenty-eight . . .'

The lady took the receiver from him. 'The street is called Gulevej, Charlottenlund. Your son is safe here, at number thirty-six. I'll ring off now and keep him here.'

Then her husband came, supporting Rasmus. Chris pulled himself together and smiled weakly. 'Hi!'

Rasmus said 'Hi' too; he was looking quite done in.

'This is Rasmus,' Chris explained. 'They kidnapped him so that his father wouldn't talk – he knew two of them slightly.'

Rasmus was given cognac as well and he coughed and spluttered. But it did help; you felt more normal after it, just a bit funny in the head.

In next to no time Father was there, and Mother and Jørgen.

'Hello,' said Chris. 'I'm all right . . . honestly. This is Rasmus . . . We helped each other.'

There was something he had forgotten – if only his voice would obey him.

'Father! "Miasmal" – I bet you never thought of that!'

Mother made a stifled sound and then they were all three blowing their noses . . .

It was absolutely wonderful to be home. The lamps were lit and there was tea and sandwiches, just as if it were still that evening when he had not come home from the chess club; only Rasmus was here too, with a bandage round his leg, and his own hand was expertly bound as well. The policeman had just gone after having heard everything they could tell him. That is, Chris had talked . . . Rasmus had had to have every word dragged out of him. But at least he hadn't protested about anything Chris had said. Now there was only his father left . . .

There he was: the doorbell had rung.

'Oh, you're Rasmus' father, aren't you?' Chris said quickly, before Mr Møller could get beyond saying 'Good evening'. 'He's a bit leftish himself, you see, so he knew one of them and got suspicious, so they kidnapped Rasmus . . .'

It wasn't a particularly good story, it needed a lot of embroidery. Mr Møller said nothing, but just looked at Father, who looked gravely back at him.

'I've already talked to Mr Møller, Chris,' said Father.

Oh cripes! Was he going to confess now and be noble at Mrs Møller's and Tina's expense? Chris looked at his mother. 'Rasmus has a little sister too, and, Mother, his mother makes frightfully good home-made bread – Rasmus says,' he added hastily.

Mr Møller's face was as furrowed as the trees in a fairy-tale wood. He gave a little tired, strangely sad smile. 'You shouldn't believe everything people say, Christopher.'

'Are you lying, Christopher?' his father asked, quite calmly.

Chris looked straight into his eyes. He could feel his face burning. 'No!' he said firmly.

The three grown-ups looked at each other for an endless moment, while Chris held his breath and Rasmus gnawed at his thumb.

Then Chris's father said slowly: 'We can usually rely on what Chris says.'

And that, just as he had told the first tall story of his life! Cripes!

I AM DAVID

Anne Holm

'David lay quite still in the darkness of the camp, waiting for the signal.

"You must get away tonight," the man had told him. "Stay awake so that you're ready just before the guard is changed. When you see me strike a match, the current will be cut off and you can climb over – you'll have half a minute for it, no more."'

Silent and watchful, David, the boy from the camp, tramps across Europe, knowing that at any moment they may catch up with him.

'. . . the boy's strange, intense, self-preserving view of life is realised superbly.'

The Sunday Times

'A most compassionate, powerful, moving book, full of hope and tenderness.'

The Evening Standard

THE TRIAL OF ANNA COTMAN

Vivien Alcock

Thin, sallow and nosy, Lindy Miller is the most unpopular girl in the school. They only let her join the Society of Masks because she was Jeremy Miller's kid sister. When a new girl arrives, the quiet, smiling Anna Cotman, Lindy persuades her to join the Society too. Originally set up to combat bullying, the Society of Masks has become a sinister power group run by bullies. When the gentle Anna challenges their rules, the leaders decide to make an example of her and the terrifying countdown to the day of her trial begins.

Vivien Alcock captures the chilling mood of evil let loose in a school when childish rituals run out of control.

CRISIS ON CONSHELF TEN

Monica Hughes

When Moon-born, fifteen year old Kepler Masterman visits Earth for the first time, he finds heavy gravity impossible to live in. An underwater atmosphere seems to offer the best solution to his problems and friendly relatives welcome him to their experimental community many fathoms deep in the depths of the ocean. But on Conshelf Ten Kepler discovers a sinister situation linked to the mysterious, water-breathing Gillmen, and realises that not only is he in great personal danger but that the survival of the entire Earth is threatened.

'Strangely convincing.'

Daily Telegraph

'An excellent story.'

The Times

THE HAUNTING

Margaret Mahy

'When, suddenly, on an ordinary Wednesday, it seemed to Barney that the world tilted and ran downhill in all directions, he knew he was about to be haunted again.'

Tabitha can't help noticing the change in Barney – how quiet he's become, his pale expression and those dazed eyes which seem to be seeing things from another world. But as Tabitha determines to solve the mystery she finds herself in very deep waters. Who was Barney's Great-Uncle Cole? Is he really dead? And who can save Barney from the terrifying experiences which seem to be taking hold of him?

'Strong and terrifying . . . The novel winds up like a spring. A psychological thriller."
Times Literary Supplement

FRIEND OR FOE

Michael Morpurgo

The Germans are bombing London. They killed
David's father. Every day people are dying in the
Blitz. David and Tucky have had to leave their
London homes and live with strangers out in the
country. They hate all Germans; everyone does.

But when David is drowning, it's a German
soldier who rescues him:

'He saved your life,' Tucky says. 'You owe him,
Davey. We both do.'

THE FOX HOLE

Ivan Southall

'"*Where?* I can't see you." Hugh's voice hadn't come any closer and sounded almost frightened . . .

"I don't know where. Over here. You can hear me, can't you? You must know where I am."

Hugh didn't say anything. Hugh didn't answer . . .

"Hugh," Ken called.

"*Help me!*"

"I can't."

"*Why?*"

Hugh suddenly cried out. "You shouldn't have gone there. Not in the gully. No one ever goes there . . . Even the dogs won't. I don't know why, but no one ever goes there . . ."'

Ken had been looking forward to this holiday weekend with his cousins for months. But on the first night he gets trapped in an old mine-shaft with a sinister history, and from that moment the tension and excitement become unbearable. And neither Ken nor any of the others will ever be the same again . . .

DREAM FOR DANGER

Anna Lewins

Todd and Tessa are used to aliens – New London is full of them, and so is their school. But Gilen and Luz are different. More mysterious and more powerful than any other children Todd and Tessa have ever met, there is trouble from the moment they arrive. The Betrayer, their enemy, has been waiting for them . . .

As summer is turned into winter the battle has begun. And the only way the children can stop everything from being destroyed is to go to the frozen heart of the now deserted capital, Old London, and find the Betrayer himself.

PARCHMENT HOUSE

Cara Lockhart Smith

From the outside Parchment House looks like any other house. But, home for the orphans of Carstairs and Bungho, it holds dark and sinister secrets. And, like the other orphans in the house, Johnnie Rattle is all alone in the world . . .

Governed by the worthies, the children live a life of drudgery maintaining the gadgets designed to make their superiors more comfortable. But when the 'ultimate' gadget arrives life at Parchment House becomes intolerable. Archibald, a huge and gleaming robot, is programmed to control, discipline and educate the children. But when Archie's cruelty becomes too much for the orphans, Johnnie Rattle has the courage to instigate a rebellion. He risks everything to save the children . . .

In PARCHMENT HOUSE, her first novel, Cara Lockhart Smith has created a nightmare world where good triumphs over evil. It is a wonderfully funny, original and touching fantasy.

HOMECOMING

Elsa Posell

Life was always good for the Koshansky family until the Revolution. Overnight, their lives change beyond belief. Distrusted and discriminated against, the family crumbles. Father flees the country and their home becomes a headquarters for the Bolshevik soldiers.

Mother tries to hold her family together but will they survive the cruel winter? Will they ever escape from Russia?

The extraordinary story of a family's fight against oppression and persecution.

THE RED PONY

John Steinbeck

Ten year old Jody can hardly believe his eyes when his father presents him with his own pony, a red colt which he calls Gabilan after the grand and pretty mountains near the ranch. Jody longs for the time when he can ride Gabilan, but he knows there are months of training ahead. The old ranch hand Billy Buck knows more than anyone else about horses and their care, but one day he makes a mistake – with tragic consequences for Jody and his red pony.

Full of vivid detail about the life of a rancher's son almost half-a-century ago, THE RED PONY is the story of a young boy growing in wisdom and understanding through his experience of loss. First published in 1938 it is a story of timeless appeal, written with the richness of language and economy of style that mark John Steinbeck's finest work.

STARRY NIGHT
FRANKIE'S STORY
BEAT OF THE DRUM

Catherine Sefton

Catherine Sefton's moving trilogy shows how the political and social situation in Northern Ireland affects young people on both sides of the divide at critical moments in their lives. Each book considers different viewpoints: the disturbing truth behind the crisis in Kathleen's family (STARRY NIGHT); the trouble encountered by the unconventional Catholic, Frankie, who has a Protestant boyfriend (FRANKIE'S STORY); and finally a look at loyalist Protestants through the eyes of young, crippled, Brian Hanna (BEAT OF THE DRUM).

VOYAGE OF QV66

Penelope Lively

It was because of Stanley the voyage began. Pal the dog, Ned, Offa, Freda the cow and Pansy all knew what kinds of animals they were, but no one had ever seen anything like Stanley.

In a flooded world, from which humans have fled, this animal band voyages from Carlisle to London to find out just what Stanley is. Their only clue is a poster from London Zoo.

'brilliant comedy layered with meaning for many ages and tastes . . . Pathos, wit, suspense and intellectual toughness combine in Penelope Lively's superbly entertaining novel.'

Margery Fisher, *Sunday Times*

'For us, anyway, this is *the* Children's Book of the Year'

Books for your Children

A Selected List of Fiction from Mammoth

☐	416 13972 8	**Why the Whales Came**	Michael Morpurgo £2.50
☐	7497 0034 3	**My Friend Walter**	Michael Morpurgo £2.50
☐	7497 0035 1	**The Animals of Farthing Wood**	Colin Dann £2.99
☐	7497 0136 6	**I Am David**	Anne Holm £2.50
☐	7497 0139 0	**Snow Spider**	Jenny Nimmo £2.50
☐	7497 0140 4	**Emlyn's Moon**	Jenny Nimmo £2.25
☐	7497 0344 X	**The Haunting**	Margaret Mahy £2.25
☐	416 96850 3	**Catalogue of the Universe**	Margaret Mahy £1.95
☐	7497 0051 3	**My Friend Flicka**	Mary O'Hara £2.99
☐	7497 0079 3	**Thunderhead**	Mary O'Hara £2.99
☐	7497 0219 2	**Green Grass of Wyoming**	Mary O'Hara £2.99
☐	416 13722 9	**Rival Games**	Michael Hardcastle £1.99
☐	416 13212 X	**Mascot**	Michael Hardcastle £1.99
☐	7497 0126 9	**Half a Team**	Michael Hardcastle £1.99
☐	416 08812 0	**The Whipping Boy**	Sid Fleischman £1.99
☐	7497 0033 5	**The Lives of Christopher Chant**	Diana Wynne-Jones £2.50
☐	7497 0164 1	**A Visit to Folly Castle**	Nina Beachcroft £2.25